THE POWER AND THE BLOOD

BOOKS BY TABITHA BAUMANDER

ELSEWHERE
THE POWER AND THE BLOOD

THE POWER AND THE BLOOD

TABITHA BAUMANDER

SPEAKING VOLUMES, LLC

NAPLES, FLORIDA

2011

THE POWER AND THE BLOOD

ISBN 978-1-61232-011-3

Library of Congress Control Number: 2010942882

CHAPTER 1

It was June 1943. The sky was blue and the weather perfect. It was just warm enough to make a working man feel glad he was alive. Softening the warmth was a sea breeze holding the perfume of faraway places.

After months of preparations in the Philadelphia shipyards the experiment was on schedule. Looking a little like a child's oversized science fair project two huge generators were mounted on the forward deck of the U.S.S. Eldridge, a destroyer escort. The generators were wired to the craft's metal structure and were ready, awaiting only the preordained time.

On the ship, seamen and officers went about their usual duties. They were aware they were involved in something special but they were only passive participants in this scientific adventure. While most working on deck and below kept this odd addition to their ship and its purpose in mind they simply concentrated on taking care of business. They were seamen and their loyalty was to their captain, craft and country. Scientists with nutty ideas might be useful and even save lives but they didn't really deserve much attention or chatter. The captain wouldn't approve.

On shore, and in small boats floating at safe distances, scientists and navy authorities watched the ship and radar operators watched their screens. World War two was at its height. Out on the seas around the world ships, men and vital supplies were being lost.

Some nameless faceless government scientist had proposed a theory to the admiralty. The radar making their ships sitting ducks to prowling German submarines could be blocked or beaten by equipping ships with powerful generators that would create a magnetic field around a ship. Theoretically this field would render a ship invisible on any radarscope. They were about to put his idea to a large and practical test.

A pretest run had been done with a selection of animals in cages. It had not been entirely satisfactory.

A green fog had covered the ship and it appeared to vanish for a moment from radar screens. It was a result that delighted the scientists and watching officials. However, boarding the ship afterward they learned that all was not right. The condition of the test animals they left in their cages on the deck had been listed in the reports euphemistically as less than optimal. But this was war and they had no time for niceties.

The animals were carefully and quietly taken away for tests and plans were made for the next step. They had to try it with people. The necessary preparations for this more complex version of the experiment were completed with quick military efficiency. There was nothing else left to be done.

Captain John Dundern stood on the bridge and looked out at his craft. The sun hung in a near cloudless sky. The sea was calm. He didn't like the idea one bit but it was almost time to turn on the power.

Like the rest of his crew he had a general idea of what they were trying to accomplish and what they would theoretically experience. Unlike his crew John Dundern also knew exactly how complex was the science involved in that effort. He also knew the condition of the animals brought off the ship after the first test. He had seen active service and considered himself far from a coward but there was a difference between bravery and foolishness.

The day before he had expressed his concerns very firmly to his superior.

"Admiral, war time or not I am having serious problems with the way we are rushing things here. Sir, some of those animals were dead. Even if it does work, killing off half my crew to avoid having the enemy do the same thing doesn't sound to me like an efficient use of resources."

The admiral had said nothing. His face said a great deal. John Dundern had served under this man for a full five years and knew how to read his commanders moods. He also knew that even admirals had to answer to someone. As if to confirm John's assumptions the admiral had very little choice in the matter the man had simply turned to the two scientists present at this last minute meeting and said,

"You're opinions gentlemen?"

They were three words that said a great deal. His commander had doubts of his own and probably a lot more information to back up those doubts. In spite of this someone higher up had ordered this test take place.

Lacking any choice in the matter he was handing the work of convincing his subordinate himself he was going to pass on the job to the two scientists who were present. They did this with the self-assured confidence of men who would be watching the action from a very comfortable distance.

"You are mistaken captain I admit to some anomalies however none of the animals were actually dead. I assure you, you and your men are in no danger," said the first.

His partner continued the thought without a pause.

"We have taken the test results into account and have adjusted our equipment accordingly."

Captain Dundern frowned remembering the complex explanation following that self-assured promise. He didn't know why he mistrusted the men who had given him the impromptu lecture. He'd gone to university on an ROTC scholarship eventually taking his master's degree with a physics major. If it weren't for the war there was a good chance he would have been wearing a lab coat himself. In spite of this he did not like what was happening.

The voice of the ship's pilot interrupted his distracting musings.

"All systems ready Captain. Power up to full. One minute to time," said the man in his usual matter of fact voice.

Captain Dundern smiled slightly. This was a man that could relay orders in the same voice whether they were on a calm smooth ocean or in the middle of a battle. Just for a moment Dundern wondered if he was displaying the same steady nerve in the face of scientific suicide.

"Very well pilot. Go on time, not before. We don't want to catch anyone off guard."

The captain looked out the forward window at the deck. He studied the two generators and wondered if he could ever get used to the presence of the great anomalous metal lumps. He imagined if the things worked he could, but right now they just looked like twin cancers begging for removal.

A movement drew his eyes and he noticed a crewman walking the deck busy doing one of the millions of things that needed to be done on a ship. He knew every man on his small ship by name but for the moment he could not think of this one. All his memory could come up with was a picture of the man hunched over a bible. He was not usually a praying man himself but he never stood in the way of anything that gave a person comfort.

The man in charge of the power switch had begun a count down. Listening to this captain Dundern wondered if the sailor he watched should be warned away from the edge of the deck. The electrical field that would theoretically render them invisible to radar could just possibly give the man a nasty shock. An electric shock victim that fell over board could easily drown before he was fished out of the drink.

"twenty,,,nineteen,,,eighteen,,,"

The Captain shook his head. Shock risk or not there was no time to get any word to the distant sailor. That man had paused in his progression and was standing and looking at the shipyards. Perhaps he was thinking of shore leave past or future. The common every day thoughts of any seaman.

"ten,,,nine,,,eight,,,"

The far off sailor's eyes moved from the shore to a gull that hovered over the ship and moved out to sea. Watching the graceful movement of the bird himself John Dundern smiled, feeling a kinship with the young bird watcher. Life on the water had its advantages even in the navy.

The captain's smile turned to a puzzled frown as he noticed this man was carrying something unusual. He quickly put it on. It was a life vest.

"five,,,four,,,three,,,"

The captain had only a moment to wonder why?

"two,,,one,,,POWER ON!"

*****

Frank Delany sat at the edge of the pier and let his legs dangle in midair. He opened his lunch box. Working the docks was a hard unforgiving life but sometimes on good days like this Frank knew he wouldn't take a cushy factory job if you gave it to him. Curiously he didn't have the stomach to go to sea himself. It was an old family joke that he sometimes felt queasy simply taking the fairy to Cony Island. But working here by the water that was the best.

He chewed his bologna sandwich heavy on the mustard and looked out at the sea and the passing ship traffic. Ships made him think of his brother-in-law somewhere in the pacific. As always he said a small prayer for his safe return. Frank knew a lot of men who complained their sisters had married bums. His sister had married one of life's' good guys. All he had to do was come home.

Frank poured a drink of coffee from his thermos and breathed in the aroma thankful that his asthma was cooperating and his lungs seemed to want to do the job for which they were intended. It was a condition that had kept him out of the army. Some days, like today when the sun was out and the air smelt of freedom, he was glad.

Frank drank some coffee and looked out at the water. Something was there floating on the waves. First it looked like a log. Then it looked like something that made his stomach turn to ice. Stiffly he climbed to his feet and began waving for attention.

Hey. Hey! Somebody, anybody, come here! Is that what I think it is? I'll be damned if it doesn't look like a body!" he called.

Men came running and he was quickly surrounded by a small crowd including Tim Smith his foreman, a stout balding man with half a life time on the docks under his belt. Next to his foreman stood the Max Jenson, captain of a tugboat moored at the dock. Jenson stuck his tongue in one cheek and squinted at the distant sight.

"I think your right it is a body. In fact I'm sure of it. We gotta get out there before the current grabs it and pulls it out to sea."

"Can you get it in the tug Max?" asked Frank.

Jenson shook his head and said, "We're not working today, engine trouble. Come on I think we can get it with our dingy."

"I'm coming," Frank said.

He shoved his thermos and sandwich into his lunch box then put the lunch box into his foreman's hands for safekeeping. Leaving the surprised man to simply watch him go he and followed the tug captain to the rowboat that floated in the water behind the tug. Letting Frank do the job of casting off and pushing them away from the tug. Max sat in the rowers seat grabbed the ores and pulled hard moving the small boat with a speed that forced Frank to simply hang on.

He was no seaman, but he knew why he was here. It was a bit selfish but he'd seen the body first. This was his scrap of excitement and he wanted to be in on the tale till the end.

Keeping his eye on their goal Frank gave Max directions at the same time willing his stomach to behave and let him have this little bit of glory untarnished. Within minutes they were sitting in the water directly beside the floating body.

"Holly crap Max, he's alive," Frank said.

Max leaned forward slightly and nodded. The tug captain had been on the water for most of his life. Frank knew he'd seen just about everything and at this point. There was very little left that could excite or upset his composure.

He said, "Yeah you're right. Okay Frank this is going to be tricky. I know you're not much of a boatman so you need to do just what I tell you when I tell you to do it. Make a mistake and you'll tip us over instead of pulling him in."

The tug captain pulled in his ores and retrieved a long pole with a hook from the bottom of the little boat. He reached out with this pole and hooked the floating man pulling him toward their little craft. The floating man moved with as little effort as a leaf on a stream.

"He's navy. They must have had some kind of accident up at the yard," Max muttered.

"I guess so." Frank agreed. "But, how the hell did he get all the way over here? Even if he fell out without anyone noticing right away shouldn't they have started looking for him and fished him out before he got this far?"

Carefully they inched the waterlogged man into the rowboat. He was an ordinary able seaman wearing a life vest. It was the thing that had kept him alive.

"Usually yeah," Max muttered. "Sometimes things happen that ain't usual."

Frank looked up from the semiconscious man moving sluggishly at the bottom of the boat and found something he never thought he'd see. Impossibly the rough dock hardened tug captain looked almost afraid.

"What's wrong Max you look like you seen a ghost?" Frank asked.

Max glanced toward the distant military installation then busied himself with his ores. He turned the boat around and they started in to shore. When he spoke his eyes were dark and full of worry.

He said, "Guy I know, no one special just a wharf rat, said something happened there yesterday. This guy might have been part of that something. That's why he got this far this boy's been in the water since yesterday."

Frank looked from the tug captain to the waterlogged sailor. The man in front of him had seen action in the last war. He had taken his boat out into hurricanes to rescue ships. He had civilian and military medals to mark his bravery and had even had his picture in the paper. Yet it was clear this man was in the grip of an uncertain fear.

"What was it?" Frank asked.

"I'm not sure I want to tell you," Max said.

The sailor began to mumble something about the eyes of god. Frank didn't think anything of it, being in the water for almost a full day, even if you probably did spend most of it out cold, would cause anyone to see god.

"What could a wharf rat learn that was so terrible?" Frank asked.

"This guy's an old friend from the last war but the drink got him. He gets the DT's sometimes and knows what a nut wagon looks like from the outside and the inside," began the captain.

Frank shrugged and said, "Yeah, so? It happens. Life gets to you. I got a cousin like that, what's the connection?"

"They had ten wagons, military wagons, parked over there and they were loading sailors into them. These were guys off the Eldrige. Frank, they were stark staring mad. There were others too. Those ones were covered up like there were dead!"

The young man, barely older than seventeen, lying in the bottom of the boat slowly opened his eyes. He turned his head stiffly taking in where he was and who he was with. He began to speak but Frank wasn't sure if he was speaking to his rescuers or himself.

"They opened the door to heaven. I doubted their wisdom. I was unworthy."

By the time they reached the dock the young man was aware enough to sit up in the boat and with help climb the ladder to the dock. He did so to the cheers of the watching dock-workers. The war had shown them all far too much darkness. A soggy seventeen year old kid was more than a cause for celebration. Here the Tim Smith took charge shooing away all but the tugboat captain and Frank.

"All right you bums shows over. We got cargo to move. Get yer lazy asses back to work lunch is over."

With Tim leading the way Max and Frank helped the boy to the nearby warehouse and sat him on a wooden chair. A rough wool blanket generally used to wrap delicate objects during shipping was wrapped around his shivering form.

"You relax sailor I'll call your people, they'll come to get you. You'll be just fine. Frank you got any coffee left in that thermos?"

The foreman pointed toward Franks lunch box left on a crate. Frank spared a quick thought to his only half eaten lunch then pushed the thought from his mind. Lots of guys on this dock worked whole days with nothing in their bellies. When money was short you fed the kids first and when some kid's half dead and shivering the hot drink goes to him.

"Yeah, sure plenty," he said.

Frank pulled out his thermos and brought it back to where the sailor sat dripping.

"They don't know what they've done. They have opened the doors to heaven," the boy said.

Tim Smith stared blankly at the babbling sailor. He shook his head and looked to his companions.

"What the hell's he talking about?" he asked. "Did he say anything in the boat? There had to have been an accident over at the shipyard or something."

Frank looked from the thermos in his hands to the tug boat captain who shook his head slightly. Frank knew what he meant. Some sea stories were just not meant for sharing.

"I don't think we wanna know boss," Frank said.

The wet sailor stared ahead as if looking at not a thing but at a single pure thought. When he spoke, a shiver went down Frank's spine. It was madness.

"A door opened can be opened again. A door to heaven opened by a live and living man."

Suddenly the teen threw off the blanket and dashed through the warehouse toward a door that would lead to the street. The foreman took a step to follow but was stopped by Max Jenson.

"No! We don't want to follow Tim. In fact I don't think this never happened," Jenson said firmly.

Smith pulled out of Jenson's grip and pointed in the direction the sailor had fled.

"What do you mean never happened?" he yelled. "That boy is sick!"

"I know!" said Max. "I know he is."

The captain paused as if desperately searching for the words that would make the man in front of him understand. He rubbed a hand over his stubble covered chin then ran it through his inch long graying hair. He made a face as if the act of willing a decent man to go against his instincts was more than painful.

"The navy did something to make him that way and I don't think the navy likes outsiders to know about their mistakes. I heard about something that happened. The sort of thing they lock you up for in wartime if you know. They might even lock you up for knowing this if there wasn't a war," Max said.

Tim Smith swallowed hard and looked from one man to the other. Understanding slowly showed in his face. It was a face pale with apprehension and at the same time flushed with anger. It was common knowledge the

9

military had secrets. It was also common knowledge they didn't like to share those secrets with just anyone.

"Oh shit," he said. "You really think it's like that?"

Frank studied his boss's face and suspected his own was just as troubled. They were good men struggling with the demons of human compassion and self-interest and they hated themselves just a little for the choice they knew they had to make. The captain had already made his choice but he stood looking at his friends willing them to be strong.

"I guess they'll find him," Tim said reluctantly. "Who'd miss a guy soaking wet and wandering around talking like a nut?"

"Boss, I don't think this ever happened," said Frank. "I think maybe the guy floated to shore on his own and walked through here when no one was looking. I mean the boys out there saw us pull a guy from the water but maybe it was just an ordinary merchant seaman. He left when we weren't looking. A lot of those guys they wear uniforms just like the regulation navy."

Max Jenson smiled at this creative solution. He gave Frank an approving nod.

"You know Frank I think that's exactly how it happened," said Max. "Boys you know my history. Back in the last war I had a couple of missions, more than a couple truth be told. If I told you about them I'd get locked up even now. The navy, the army, they like to keep their secrets, secret."

Tim Smith thought a long moment then nodded his head slightly. His shoulders slumped in the face of some weight much heavier than the biggest crate on the docks.

He said, "I'll be in my office. Frank don't worry about what time you finish your lunch. You did your good deed for the day you shouldn't have to work hungry because of it."

Tim Smith walked toward his office. Watching him go the tugboat captain draped the now damp blanket over a chair to dry. Frank waited till the office door was closed before speaking.

"So you think the navy will just pick him up?" he wondered out loud.

Captain Max nodded. He led the way back to the door to the warehouse. The day was still bright and warm and beautiful. Deep inside Frank's chest sat a cold and bitter stone.

"Oh sure. Or the cops will and they'll call the navy. There's no doubt he's got his brains scrambled Frank, but who knows if it's permanent. Anyway he needs help and if they did it to him then they can damn well undo it!"

CHAPTER 2

John Denning a slightly balding man in his late forties sat at his desk in shirtsleeves. His tie was pulled loosely and his sport jacket hung on the back of his chair. On the whole he looked middle of the week, middle of the day casual. The smile on his face was holiday weekend wide.

"In this day and age this last part isn't strictly speaking necessary but some traditions exist for a reason. Even if it's just to have proof to hold in your hands," he said.

Reaching into the bottom drawer of his desk he pulled out an ink pad and a stamp. He inked the stamp and applied it to the papers in front of him. THUMP! THUMP! THUMP! He then folded the papers and handed them across the desk.

"Here you go Miss Anderson. One mortgage paid in full."

Claire Anderson took the folded papers from her bank manager. She sat for a moment in the chair in front of his desk looking at the "PAID IN FULL", stamp. The hand that held the papers trembled slightly. Some traditions did indeed exist for a reason and the vision in her hands was a beautiful thing.

She was divorced, just thirty-five and not only inexplicably able to earn a living in her chosen vocation but had just paid off her recently purchased house. The man she sat across from seemed to understand completely.

"Not many people I know pay off their house in three years. Going to have a mortgage burning party?" he asked.

Claire looked across the desk at the bank manager and smiled. John was leaning back in his chair one hand toying with the stamp. The other closed the ink pad with a casual click. Around them the business of the bank went on as usual but it was clear he was enjoying this moment almost as much as she was and appeared to be in no hurry to get on to other matters.

"Burn it? Hell no. I may frame the thing. Forget how long it did or didn't take, do you know how few people in my generation are going to see PAID IN FULL on a mortgage?"

"Actually I do," said the bank manager dryly.

The pleased sparkle in the man's eye dulled slightly.

He said, "Houses are so expensive these days it's almost impossible for most people to finish paying for the things in one generation. That's why I wanted to handle this bit of business myself. The prerogative of being the boss."

Claire slipped the now defunct mortgage papers into her roomy purse. The small bundle fit nicely next between her palm pilot and her wallet. All three things swam in a sea of assorted flotsam filling the large canvass bag. She cleaned it out once a month but it always seemed to fill so very quickly.

She gave a satisfied sigh and said, "I've done a lot of money management this last couple of years. Its been wonderful, not to mention educational. A bit scary too. I keep expecting to wake up and discover the dreams over I have to go back to the day job."

John Denning took the stamp and ink pad and put them back into his lower desk drawer. He shut the drawer then leaned back in his chair showing her a wide satisfied smile. The business of the moment was finished but the bank manager seemed just as interested in his client as her business.

"I never waste ink on dream mortgages. Trust me the house is paid for and you have more than enough in the bank to keep the day job monster at bay," he said. "It's a strange but true fact that good things do tend to happen all at once. I've seen it myself."

Thinking over the events of the previous few years Claire said, "It's been a strange wild ride. I sold a screenplay, then a book. Then I sold another screenplay. When you've spent years just writing and submitting and writing some more actually selling is a whole new feeling."

"I bet it's a good one. Don't forget to let us know when the first hits theaters," Denning said.

"Don't worry I will," said Claire. "The odd thing is even though I adapted the scripts from books. Be books themselves haven't actually sold yet. Seems oddly unbalanced somehow."

Claire puzzled for a moment at the odd order in which the material sold. She started teaching herself screen writing after finishing her fifth book. It occurred to her that perhaps she wasn't really writing novels, she was writing the novelizations of screenplays that hadn't actually been written yet. True or not the logic worked and her life as a writer began.

"Oh I'm sure they'll sell," said the bank manager. "The universe craves balance."

The philosophical comment caught Claire off guard and she paused for a moment wondering if he was being either patronizing or sarcastic. It didn't take her long to deduce he was simply being confident.

She said, "My agent seems to think they will very soon. You know if I'd put it in a book I'd eventually have to edit it out. Normal reality just doesn't work like that."

Claire stood and shouldered her big bag. The manager stood and they shook hands.

"Any immediate plans for the future?" he asked.

"I think I'm going to pack my car up with the necessities of life and go for a long driving holiday. I haven't had any kind of real brake since well before this whole ride started. If it comes to that I don't think I've ever been on an actual road trip. Too busy just trying to survive. "

Claire took a step toward the office door. The manager slipped his hands in his pockets and studied her with a quizzical look in his eyes. It was a look that reminded her of the invisible wall that stood between anyone who managed to make a living, or even tried to make a living, in the arts and the vast majority of society. They might live on this same planet but in truth they were on completely different worlds.

"I wonder what a newly successful screenwriter-novelist considers a necessity?" he asked.

Claire paused at the open door and thought for a moment. Road trips were something other people took. For a moment she honestly wasn't sure what she would pack.

"Let's see. I'm never without my palm pilot. I use it for notes and ideas that hit me. I'd take my lap top computer with a utility belt full of charged batteries, my battery charger and my cell phone. After that I think you'd have to say; diet cola, M&M's, and a suitcase full of jeans and T-shirts. Of course I'd have to have one or two dresses so I can get into nice restaurants. We'll have to see about that part. Maybe I'll shop as I go."

"That's pretty basic for someone who's suddenly rather well off and due to be even better off," he said.

Claire laughed at his bemused assessment of her list.

"It depends on what you want out of life. All I ever wanted to do is write and sell what I write. The money means I don't have to worry and I can travel more, but I'm still the same person."

He settled back down behind his desk and picked up a pen. The interlude was over and clearly there was work to be done.

"Sounds very wise," he said. "Have a good trip."

Claire gave him a wide smile and turned to walk out the door and through the bank. The tellers and other bank employees gave her an ovation as she went. They all knew what she was here for and they were genuinely pleased.

These were good people, sympathetic in hard times and now delighted with her success. She waved royally as she went and just before she left the bank turned and gave a deep bow.

Leaving the bank behind her Claire Anderson walked out into the spring sunshine. Walking along the street for a moment she found a small red hatch back parked at a meter. She got in, tossed her bag into the passenger seat and drove home.

*****

The call from Jane Pendelton, her New York agent, came in the early evening after the cheap rates had taken effect. The woman was successful in her profession and in Claire's eyes very close to a miracle worker but that didn't stop her from pinching pennies. Claire was stretched out on her over stuffed sofa, watching the baseball game.

"Jane hello! You'll never guess what I did today. I paid off my mortgage."

15

She turned the sound off on the set and prepared herself for whatever message the woman wanted to impart. Claire was realistic about her relationship with this woman. Jane Pendelton was a sociable sounding person but she never phoned just to say hello to one of her authors, not even on off peak hours.

"Sweetie you're so responsible. This is incredible news," Jane said sounding remarkably sincere.

"Yep. I have a respectable cash flow. I own the roof over my head. Heck, even the car's paid for."

Claire knew she was droning on a bit and forced herself to stop. One problem with a solitary profession was it tended to limit the amount of people with which one could share good news.

"We'll have to work on our cash flow wont we," Jane said. "See if we can't move that respectable up a notch or two. From the noises I've been hearing lately I don't think that's going to be too much trouble."

Claire shook her head slightly looking to the heavens. This woman was a very good agent a shark of the New York publishing world. The problem was she had an annoying habit of forcing authors to play I've got a secret. Unfortunately the only way to get out of the trap without losing your temper was to cut to the chase and ask the obvious.

"OK so what about the two books I adapted the screenplays from. I think it would be nice if the darn things were on shelves sometime around when the films are released," Claire said.

Claire turned her attention from the ball game on the television to the glass of ice tea that sat on the coffee table just out of comfortable reach. In a close to annoying counterpoint Jane's voice chattered on. She'd get to the point eventually but there was every possibility of more than one point to get to so patience was sadly a must.

"So do a lot of other people I assure you. I think I can promise you papers to sign by the end of this month, middle of next at the latest. They want it. I know they want it and they know I know. All we really need to talk about at this point is money. It's a very delicate balance. You ask for too little and they wonder if you're worth their while. You ask for too much and they say no thanks to expensive."

The vision of the ice filled drink was too much to bare. Claire pushed herself up into a sitting position and reached for the tea.

"I will never understand publishing executives," she said, glass in hand.

"No one does dear," Jane said, for a moment the flowery tone in her voice hardened just slightly. "They're like trout you don't understand them you just learn how to play the game. You started anything new yet?"

Claire grinned at the slight tense quality that had touched the woman's voice. It was a common thing with the publishing business and Claire understood completely. If you were hot you had to make as much money as you could because there was no telling when the tide would turn. The difference between best seller and sale counter reject was painfully slim.

"Don't worry Jane it causes wrinkles. I have five more sitting on my hard disk you haven't even seen. I was writing for a long time before you picked me up you know almost ten years. I'll be keeping you busy for a while before you have to wait for anything fresh."

"Wonderful."

The woman's light bantering eagerness returned. Claire found herself smiling broadly and almost laughed at the transition. Mentally she ticked off two reasons for this phone call; let the client know an end is in sight to one annoying issue. Make sure that client has more product to sell.

"Listen, I'm glad you phoned," Claire said. "I've just about decided I want to take a little driving holiday. Down in the states, maybe the Carolinas."

The New York agent's chatty tone lost some of its casualness and slipped into strait forward business.

"Well dear, you certainly deserve a brake but how do I get in touch with you when I need you to sign papers?" she asked.

"Don't worry I wouldn't think of traveling without the lap top. And I'll have my cell phone. Just phone or send me an e-mail that its time and I'll drive on up. Or along depending on where the heck I am at the time. The idea just hit me to day honestly and I don't really know where I'm going."

Jane sighed deeply into the phone and said, "Now she's doing geography. Too much for me at this hour. There's the pizza boy. I'm off dear. I'll keep in touch."

The woman hung up the phone and Claire reached for the remote to turn the sound to the set back on. Just as she did a Toronto Blue Jay batter sent a ball into the stadium's second balcony. Home run.

*****

Claire lay on her couch in the dark silent living room staring at the ceiling. Feeling a need for fresh air she went to her front door and opened it breathing in the night. She reached for a sweater. The night air was cold and good all at once.

Looking out through the screen door at the three AM. street with its darkened houses, Claire smiled ruefully. She was hyper in the extreme and had an idea that if she got much more than an hours sleep this night she would be lucky.

Against all expectations the ride of success any writer dreams of had actually stopped long enough to let her hop on and get a seat. Barring disaster she was well on the way to becoming the sort of writer other writers interview and envy. It was scary and exciting all at once yet all she could think of was this house.

It was situated in a Toronto neighborhood called The Beaches. This was because all the north, south running streets ended at a ribbon of park land rimming this section of Lake Ontario. This meant her street had the best of both worlds, city at one end, country, or a reasonable facsimile of the country at the other.

Claire stepped out onto the verandah that lined the front of her house and looked down the street at the distant twinkle of water. The house was a small brick structure built originally as housing for factory labor some time before the First World War. To Claire it was a dream made in the shape of brick and stone and intricately cut woodwork.

The previous owner a computer executive had gone to great pains to have it renovated. Unfortunately just when the job was finished he'd been forced to sell due to a job transfer. There were two rooms and a bathroom on a small second floor and a living room dining room and kitchen that made up the ground floor. With one of the second floor rooms in use as a bedroom and the other as an office it was just about perfect.

The first screenplay sale had given her enough of an investment income to live here. The book sale had given her the down payment. The final sale, completed just weeks before, had closed the deal.

The desperate scramble for basic security and a place to belong had miraculously vanished. Even if big name fame never appeared she now had the security to be a working writer. The brain dulling routine of office and daily commute was a thing of the past.

It was time to think of what to write next. Well, soon it would be. For now it was enough to savor the victory. Like most of the best victories it had been a long time in coming.

Claire leaned against a verandah post and listened to the combinations of night sounds. From one direction came the very natural sound of water lapping on sandy beach and rocky shore. A bell from a floating buoy echoed across the dark water and a gull cried out in answer.

From the opposite came the late night sounds of cars on pavement. It was a sporadic murmur at this hour but it was there, an odd counterpoint to the natural music of water sand and gull. There was a down side to living here. The weekend traffic consisting mainly of people coming from just about anywhere in the city to go to the beach for one. But there were few other places in this city she would rather live.

An echoing electric crackle cut this subdued late night concerto. Claire looked up at the sky puzzled. It was hardly the night sky she would see out in the country but there were more than enough stars in evidence to deny the presence of even a single cloud.

"Since when do you get lightening from a cloudless sky?" she pondered.

Claire looked down the street again toward the lake. This time there was a man standing in the center of the road. Back lit by the moonlight on the water at this distance he was little more than a silhouette.

Claire took a step back away from the street and toward her open front door. Men walking around in the middle of the night were not necessarily dangerous but they weren't usually the best company either.

He began walking north still in the center of the road. Claire watched him come, attracted by a confusing stiffness in his gate. He moved as if he were pushing through thigh deep mud. He passed under the first street light and she saw that the man was totally nude!

CHAPTER 3

The man moved through the summer night like a lost soul in the grip of a dream. His face, at first made indistinct by distance, showed this dream of his was more like a nightmare. His blue eyes were wide and staring. His mouth a stiff line open slightly breathing in the cool night air.

He looked at the dark houses as if something were there to fear behind their silent locked doors. A cloud of near visible terror seemed to radiate out from him to grip her by the throat. Gasping to catch her breath Claire felt her heart begin to beat a sympathetic rhythm. She'd written about unreasoning fear, never before had she understood the concept so completely.

His hair was dark brown and very short. His clearly displayed body was well built though not in a showy way with a skin tone that ran from the creamy white outline of a swimsuit to well-tanned legs and forearms. It looked like the body of a policeman or fireman or some other profession that required strength as a matter of course.

He stopped in front of the house and Claire backed into her open door-way. She could be behind an inch thick oak door locked by a sturdy dead bolt in less time than it would take for him to get from the center of the road to the sidewalk.

He turned his head as if he spotted her movement out of the corner of his eye and saw her standing in the shadows. It seemed as if he was having problems mentally processing the fact that in this dim hour on this quiet home lined street there was actually a soul awake and watching. A light that looked like hope went on in his eyes and he opened his mouth as if to speak.

The effort seemed to do something to him. He flinched as if an electric shock were ricocheting through his system. He grabbed his head and it seemed as if he would have screamed out in agony if he had the power.

Claire stepped back out onto her verandah and down one of the three steps that would take her to the short path that cut through her front lawn and led to the sidewalk. Even in his pain he reacted to her movement jerking away from her with such force that he fell to the pavement. Claire thought for a moment he was afraid of her, then curiously she had the oddest impression that he was afraid FOR her.

"Look Mr. you just lay still," she called out. "I'll go in for a minute and phone for help. You need the police, or an ambulance, maybe both."

Listening to this the handsome face that looked up from the pavement was a picture of deep despair. The man scrambled to his feet and began a lurching half run toward the distant commercial street. Claire watched him go and knew she had to follow.

"Aw hell in for a penny in for a pound."

She dashed back to the door and reached in to grab her keys from a hook on the wall. She then locked the door and ran after this troubled shadow. She was sure now he wasn't a threat. He was simply a man in distress and she seemed to be the only human being awake and able to make an attempt at some kind of help.

In the short time it had taken her to lock the door the troubled man had gotten within twenty yards of the main street. He stood hovering in the darkness looking out at the relatively well lit avenue. It seemed as if the light and the possible presence of other people had stopped him.

Claire called to him saying, "Wander out there mister you'll get help soon enough. It's late, late enough to be early. You won't stay ignored for long."

The man spun at the sound of her voice. He was now bent over slightly and holding his hands together at the wrists. It appeared as if some just bearable pain had begun to emanate from those twin points. He looked trapped behind a wall of pain and some invisible unnamed terror.

"I'm not a day dream mister I'm really here and I really want to help. I'm sure some time in detox or something and you'll be fine. Or on your way to being fine."

Claire felt like she was babbling like an idiot. At the same time somewhere in the back of her memory was something a high school guidance councilor had told her when she'd asked how to help a troubled friend. It made sense it made sense now.

"Get the persons attention and keep 'em talking. Even if what they're saying back to you is "you're an idiot". If they're listening to you that means they've stopped focusing on other things. That all on its own can stop anyone from doing something stupid."

She had his attention all right but she wasn't sure the rest of that advice would work. Not this time. His pleading eyes met hers. His arms were now crossed across his chest as if hugging some pain. He moved one arm to examine his wrist. The wrist was red and clearly painful as if it had been tied or manacled for a long period. The wrist he hugged to his chest had the same red line. Claire tried to think of what would cause both wounds, then put the thought from her mind. She really didn't want to know.

Grasping for the magic of words again she said, "I really think a hospital or something could be a good thing. Maybe not right away but in the long run it could."

Claire approached him slowly keeping her voice soft and reassuring. One step, two steps three steps, keep talking, distract him from how close she was getting. Faintly she wondered what she would do if he did let her get within arm's reach. Filing that thought in a mental box marked --crossing that bridge when we come to it-- she took another step.

"Nice body by the way. You know I always wondered what it would be like to wander around out in the street with nothing on. Must be kind of liberating. What made you try it?"

He staggered slightly as if his legs were beginning to generate some pain of their own. Claire took a step closer and saw that like his wrists his ankles had marks of chafing from some kind of tight binding. There was one thing odd about this, odder than everything she had seen thus far. When he had stood in the road in front of her house she had looked him up and down very completely. That moment not five minutes ago his ankles had been clean and mark free.

"Where the hell did they come from?"

She said it out loud but didn't expect an answer. He was suddenly much too busy to pay attention. Enveloped some fresh wave of pain a new terror had attacked the tortured man. He looked up at some invisible point in the sky and his mouth opened in a silent scream. He broke away from the point where he had been standing and ran off the road. Again the crack of high-powered electricity cut the air. There was no mixing it up with lightning this time. It had something to do with him.

Claire ran forward knowing he could not have gone far. He had fled into a little space behind a very old synagogue. It was simply a small rectangle shaped area where the rabbi, cantor and one other worthy could park their cars.

There were only two ways he could leave this little lot. Either by a door into the small brick and stone building or by coming back out the way he had run. She had him cornered, and for the first time wished she'd thought to grab her cell phone. The man needed serious medical help.

"Olly Olly in free Adam. Eve says it's time to stop running around and go see a doctor. I'm fresh out of fig leaves but I've got an old coverall that might fit. I had a husband at one time. He never did collect all of his stuff. Kept the coverall to wear when I work on my garden, but hey, I never work on my garden so it's good as new."

The man was gone. There were no car's to hide behind. The door into the building was locked. There was no way he could not be there except he was not.

Dangling on her key chain was a small flashlight designed to help find keyholes in dark places. Claire danced the pencil thin beam of light around the space. The splinter of light confirmed what she already knew. Against all logic the man had completely vanished.

Claire backed away from the small lot. As she had when the man had stood in the center of the road Claire felt the sort of fear that before now she had only known in theory. She turned and began to walk quickly back to her home, her eyes on the shadows heart pounding. This was not fear felt in the strange abstract way that helped her turn terror into words and make it real for her readers. This was the pure childlike fear created best by the unexplained.

Claire unlocked her front door with trembling hands, closing it behind her with an echoing slam. She turned the dead bolt slumping against the door as the sound of the click followed the slam in reverberating through the house.

Safe in her small haven Claire jerked away from the door and walked deliberately to the kitchen. Flipping a switch activated the fluorescent lights in the ceiling and pushed away the night. She stood for a moment letting the utterly normal disastrous clutter grab hold of her panicked nervous system. Going to the refrigerator Claire pulled out a small half bottle of red wine. It was small, she never had been much of a drinker, but it would have to do.

"OK Claire let's check our disbelief at the door and reason this out loud. You're no journalist but you know what what's real. That's why you write fantasy cause reality sucks. He was frightened. He was in pain. Someone put him here and then did something to pull him back. It was not some strange UFO daydream it was real. You know it was real."

There was something else she knew but didn't want to admit. She said it anyway knowing it was the only way to dissipate the terrible nervous energy making every nerve in her body twitch. She'd written about terror, she'd read about terror, she had now been far too close for comfort to the real thing and there wasn't a soul she could tell.

"You know it was real like you know that poor schmuck is a prisoner somewhere and there's no way you can do anything about it."

Claire felt a sob in her throat that threatens to build into a full-fledged scream. The screw top to the small bottle was covered in foil. She removed the foil and slowly crumpled into a small ball.

"He could feel them pulling him back and he was terrified. He tried to run away from whatever it was. That is not the act of a volunteer."

Claire tossed the foil ball to the table and opened the screw top lid to the half bottle. She poured half the bottle into a large wineglass she took from a cupboard.

After a long swallow she emptied the rest of the bottle into the glass and put the empty container down on the table. Feeling the nervous energy in her body begin to dissipate Claire slumped against the kitchen table.

"Damn-it why did this have to happen? Why didn't I just go to bed and watch the late movie?"

Bringing her drink Claire climbed the steps to her bedroom already feeling the drink's desired effect. The panic had gone limp. The nervous energy had retreated into a well of dark fears.

"I can't tell anyone. I can't even put it in a book."

Claire fell onto her bed against a wall of pillows. Unsteadily she grabbed for the remote to the small set sitting on a bookcase across from her bed. On the set was an infomercial about a psychic hot line. She pressed buttons and the infomercial became an old black and white movie.

"If I put this in a book someone out there might know I didn't make it up. They'd come looking for me."

Claire felt tears drip down her cheeks. She took another deep swallow of the wine, welcoming its medicinal effect. She knew that she was still very afraid. At the same time she knew she was safe and that was going to have to be enough.

Time passed marked by the regular dropping of the level of liquid in the glass. The black and white figures on the small bedroom set began to blur. Claire put the empty wine glass on the bedside table, closed her eyes and tried to at least listen to the dialoged.

"I don't think you want to meet anyone who would do this sort of thing to somebody Claire. I don't think you do at all."

CHAPTER 4

After the horror show of the night before the bright shining morning dawned like a strange anticlimax. As she often did when she couldn't sleep at night Claire snapped awake at six o-clock. She stared numbly out her bedroom window listening to the birds and the passing traffic, knowing that even if sleep did return it would be short and waking again would be accompanied by a throbbing headache. After over an hour of this mindless drifting she reluctantly dressed in a summer shift and sandals then made her way downstairs to the kitchen. A short search of the kitchen made the next step inevitable. There wasn't a single thing in the house that could even remotely be called breakfast. For a woman whose categories of acceptable breakfast foods included reheated Hamburger Helper and peanut butter and jam sandwich this was a monumental achievement.

"I have condiments, and an onion," she grumbled. "Terrific."

Annoying though this was it gave the day a practical purpose, a thing for which Claire was immediately grateful. Mission one, go out and eat breakfast. Mission two, shop for food.

After those two items another two chores set themselves up for consideration. The first involved going to the auto club and picking up a selection of maps for her proposed driving trip. The last thing to do was something she didn't like but could not avoid. She had to somehow forget the silent plea for help given by that middle of the night vision.

Even as she grabbed her purse and stepped out the front door Claire knew this last item on her to-do list was going to be impossible. She remembered every curve on his body. His deep pleading blue eyes had burned themselves into her memory. She could even remember the strange tattoo on his left buttock. It had been a small piece of Irish style scrollwork, an intertwining line like a band that ran in the shape of a circle.

Walking up the street she passed the synagogue. Still bothered by the mystery of the errant nudist's disappearance she looked into the lot and was stilled in her tracks. As it had been hours before the little lot was empty. However the small unremarkable space was not, without interest.

Someone had placed a black silhouette on the brick wall of the synagogue. The shame was very clearly the silhouette of a man with his arms extended wide. Stunned by this strange graffiti Claire left the sidewalk to examine it closely. Here was proof that the vision of the night before had been no nightmare. Or was it?

While Claire stood in front of the surreal man shaped blot an old car pulled into the lot beside her. A casually dressed man of about thirty got out of the car closed the door and leaned on the roof studying the picture. His sharp eyes were deep brown much like the brown of his closely trimmed beard. A small rainbow colored yarmulke was pinned to his head of short curly hair. He nodded hello and then stared at the wall a bemused smile on his face.

"That's a first I must say."

"You don't know the half of it," Claire muttered.

He locked his car door then circled around to stand in front of the strange image. Studying the wall a look of confusion replaced his initial amusement and a small frown replaced the smile. The confusion caught Claire off guard. She was about to ask what other than the obvious was wrong when he explained himself.

"I've seen all kinds of scribbling on synagogues and churches and this is probably the strangest," he said. "What is this stuff?"

He stepped close to the wall and took a sideways view of the image. The move pulled Claire's attention away from the figure on the wall to the man in front. She would have expected anger or annoyance not analysis.

"It's actually a good millimeter thick in spots. You know, it almost looks like wood ash or something soaked in black paint then sprayed on somehow," he observed energetically.

He shrugged in confusion then stepped away from the wall. Looking at Claire he smiled and extended his hand. The act caught her off guard and she had to hurry to return the gesture.

"I should introduce myself. I'm Alan Rose itinerant rabbi."

His grip was firm and strong. He might have been a rabbi but Claire had an idea he was not a stranger to working with his hands. A man with a demanding vocation and a practical turn of mind, she liked the combination.

"Claire Anderson, formerly itinerant writer," she said by way of introduction.

"I beg your pardon?" he asked, puzzled by the statement.

"I'm a novelist/screenwriter. I've had some luck lately and just paid off the mortgage on my house. I don't know I guess I'm still buzzed about it I only finalized things yesterday. I'm down the street, old factory housing with the roses in front."

He gave her a broad smile and seemed to genuinely understand.

"Mazle tov! That's a beautiful little place. You have every right to be excited I know I would be. Are you Jewish?"

The question caught her completely off guard.

"Actually yes," she said.

"Good then you can stay for morning prayers and after the old boys club leaves you can tell me what you know about our interesting scribble."

Claire blinked hard at the commanding confidence with which he usurped her plans for the morning. Without waiting for her to comment he pulled a well packed key ring from a pants pocket then went to the back door of the building searching the ring for the right key.

"Stand there and don't let anyone touch it," he said. "Don't touch it yourself either. What you don't know can hurt you if you're not careful."

He disappeared into the building and in a few minutes reappeared with a bucket, dustpan and small brush. Setting the bucket down in front of the strange wall picture he brushed tentatively at the strange substance. Behaving just like wet ash, it fell off the wall and onto the dustpan in large clumps. Watching this man put dustpan after dustpan full of black matter into the bucket Claire began to feel the silence uncomfortable and searched for something to say.

"You're good at that. You do windows?"

"HA! You laugh! You'd be surprised how many ways a guy finds to pay the bills while going to rabbinical school, or afterward for that matter. Although personally given a choice I lean toward carpentry."

He was almost finished before Claire spoke again.

"What makes you think I know anything about this?"

"Just a hunch. You seem like a basically honest person and you stayed when I asked you to. I also heard what you muttered just now about not knowing the half of it."

Claire stifled a laugh.

"You got me, guilty as charged."

"Hey, I'm good. You should hear me catching bar mitzvah students fibbing about doing their homework."

The rabbi straightened up and surveyed his work. There was still a faint trace of the silhouette left but most of the substance had been moved from wall to bucket. He put the dustpan on top of the bucket hiding what was inside then brushed at the wall. In seconds all traces of the strange picture were gone.

"Why didn't you want me to touch the stuff? How could it be dangerous?"

Alan Rose turned to her and shrugged. He studied the small bits that were still sticking to the brush.

"I haven't the slightest idea but, if you don't know what something is then it makes sense to take simple precautions. If I had a face mask I'd have worn that too."

"Good morning rabbi."

The sudden greeting caused both Claire and Alan to jump. The man who delivered the greeting stood on the sidewalk watching them. He was in his mid-fifties, a velvet bag holding his prayer shawl was tucked under one arm. He looked at the young rabbi and then he looked at Claire and smiled.

Claire felt her cheeks turn bright pink. Seeing their audience Alan Rose cleared his throat and picked up the bucket.

"Mr. Applebaum this is Claire Anderson. Claire and I have some business to conduct later but for now she's going to join us for prayers."

"A pleasure Miss Anderson," he said warmly.

Mr. Applebaum smiled again and continued into the building. As if rooted to the spot both Alan and Claire followed him with their eyes till he entered the building using his own key. Claire opened her mouth but Alan shushed her silently. They stayed like that till the door closed with a silent thump. At the same moment Alan made a face that caused Claire to stifle a laugh.

"Sorry about that. A single rabbi is something of an oddity. You would-n't believe the amount of introductions I get."

Claire found herself giggling quietly.

"That's OK no harm done. I'm more concerned about this morning pray-ers business. I've never done that before. Heck I hardly ever go on Saturday. My family was always pretty, well, casual."

Allan gave her a knowing look. He rolled his eyes slightly and nodded toward the door.

"Right like I haven't heard that before," he said with a kind of playful seriousness. "In."

Leading the way Alan walked her down a set of stairs through a small basement common room past a kitchen to where he put the bucket and cleaning things into a closet. It was then he noticed she was genuinely apprehensive.

"Hey chill, it won't hurt honest."

Several other men entered the synagogues rear door. Alan greeted them by name introducing them each to Claire. They greeted her in an echo of the reaction given by Mr. Applebaum and passed by to reach a set of stairs that would lead to the sanctuary.

"It won't take long at least half of these men still run businesses and need to get going after we're finished."

He then led the way up some stairs to the entrance to the sanctuary. There he stopped and handed her a circular piece of lace with a bobby pin stuck through it that was sitting next to a box full of men's head coverings, or Yarmulkes and a prayer book.

"You put that on your head. You hold this thing the right way up. You say "amen" when everyone else does. Nothing could be simpler."

*****

A short time later Claire found herself finally eating breakfast. Only instead of a restaurant it was in the synagogue's basement kitchen. She was sitting on a well-worn kitchen chair and sharing toasted bagels and tea with Alan Rose. She was also sharing what had happened to her the night before. It had started with a few reluctant admissions but once she truly began the entire story came flooding out in a torrent of words. She finished the tale and waited for him to comment. He did so only after a long and thoughtful pause.

He leaned back in his chair then let the front legs fall to the floor with a soft thump. His ever expressive brows rose slightly when he spoke.

"That's quite a story."

"I promise you it's completely true," she said. "It happened."

The expressive brows settled and his face as a whole resolved itself into the face of a scholar pondering a complex problem.

"Don't worry I believe you saw something. Or to be more accurate I believe you had a genuine experience. What that experience was, is the puzzle. I only wish I'd heard your story before I brushed the last bit of black matter off the wall into the dirt."

It took a moment for Claire to understand what her companion meant. Her mouth hung open for a moment at the thought.

"You mean that might have been him? I mean what's left of him," she asked.

Alan nodded reluctantly.

"I know it sounds far-fetched but there are only two other explanations that come to mind. Well, three really if you want to be hopeful," he said.

"And these explanations are?" Claire prodded.

He held a finger up, brushed some bagel crumbs off it and held it up again.

"First of all you're a woman whose imagination is well developed. A professional day-dreamer. Whether you like it or not it really could have been an unusually vivid dream. This stuff we have in the bucket is just a strange coincidence, wood ash or something applied to look like a crucifix. It's the sort of thing that's always getting scribbled on walls along with swastikas and nasty slogans. You fell asleep listening to the vandals smearing the muck on and your mind made up the rest."

He paused waiting for her reaction. Claire obliged staring into her half-drunk mug of tea. She frowned at the possibility floating there yet this man was prepared to help her think this through. She did not want the gift of his time to go to waste.

"I don't like it but I have to admit you could be right. I was pretty hyper last night. Any dream I might have had would have been pretty vivid. If I sleep walked in combination with the dream, something I did do when I was a kid that could cover all the bases. A dream analyst would probably have a field day with the symbolism but you could label the whole strange plot a freedom metaphor."

Letting her think the possibility through out loud Alan downed the last bite of his bagel and picked up his mug. He chewed thoughtfully for a moment then swallowed and continued his inventory.

"Don't get too dedicated to number one yet we haven't examined the others. The second explanation starts to get kind of off the wall. It could possibly have been some kind of holographic projection. Somebody used you as a lab rat in the interests of seeing whether their projected illusion was real enough to fool someone. That's why he didn't want you to get to close. If you did you would have been able to tell it was just an illusion. The stuff in the bucket was put on the wall after you left. Why, I don't know maybe to back up the illusion."

Claire began to feel faintly confused. She'd expected this pleasant pragmatic man to lead her along the path toward common sense reality. Instead he was giving fairy tales, the sort of thing she made a living writing, the same sort of weight as rational thought. Reluctantly she voiced what she knew was the third possibility.

"Or it could have been real and I actually saw a man who is wrapped up in some kind of teleportation experiment. Probably against his will," she said hesitantly.

Allan nodded and sighed deeply.

"Yes. The, if it looks, walks and quacks like a duck it can't be anything else, explanation. As strange as it seems I lean toward that one myself."

"You do?" asked Claire in unguarded disbelief.

His answer was quietly reasonable.

"Claire if I can believe that I talk to god every day, sure he doesn't talk back but he's busy, if I can believe that why can't I believe something like this?" he asked.

Claire downed the last of her tea and said; "Looked at it like that I'm starting to feel less like a nut and more like someone who just had the bad luck to be up and awake in the middle of the night."

Alan shook his head and said, "Claire what happened to you was inconvenient and scary. I have an elderly friend, a Holocaust survivor whose Russian grandparents when they were freshly married flipped a coin. Heads go all the way to America and make a completely new life. Tails go to Poland and live a life close to what they knew."

"Since he's a survivor I assume it came up tails," Claire said. "Yeah that what I call bad luck."

Alan shook his head and said, "Actually it came up heads. The bad luck was both grandparents were the sort of people that didn't think they could live with the change America would bring. They went to Poland. True story. I tell it to remind people how important an open mind can be."

"All right I'll consider myself duly chastised and remind myself to keep an open mind," Claire said.

After thinking for a moment she added. "When you look at the situation scientifically if our man was running away while they tried to zap him back to wherever he came from it could have gone wrong."

Alan's smiling face turned solemn.

"I know, that's why I'm sorry about just brushing away those last traces. I've read enough science and science fiction to understand that teleportation even in theory is a tricky business. If he was running when this beam or power or whatever they used hit him he could have been thrown against the wall and cremated instantly. Which means we could have on our hands the cremated remains of some poor soul that need to be dealt with respectably."

Alan Rose downed the last of his tea. He stood and put his empty mug into the kitchen's sink then began looking in cupboards both above and below the counter level.

To this statement Claire added; "Preferably without the press or anyone else finding out. These people play nasty if they know we know about them we both could be in deep trouble. What was that hopeful forth possibility?"

His head and shoulders shoved deep into a cupboard under the sink Allan said; "The human body is covered in a thick layer of skin. Our skin flakes off constantly and is replaced, the same thing with hair. So, if all the beam did was singe off the top layer of skin this man might be alive."

Claire considered this last hopeful possibility and smiled. It was a mixed hope certainly since he was likely still a prisoner but it was still a hope. So long as a prisoner was alive there could be rescue, or escape.

"You might have something there," she said. "What are you doing?"

"Aha!"

Looking and sounding victorious he backed out of the cupboard producing a large empty pickle jar with a wide lid. The jar was much larger than generally sold in the store. Claire guessed it had been left behind by a caterer.

"This should do nicely," he said.

Standing Alan put the big jar on the counter. He looked over at the table where Claire still sat.

"You're going to put the stuff in there?" she asked.

"I am. Then later today I'll take it to an old friend of mine. He runs a lab. I'll get him to analyze the stuff. That way we'll know if we're just telling each other horror stories."

Claire stood and put her mug in the sink.

"You won't tell him what I saw will you?"

Alan hefted up the pickle jar with both hands and led the way to the closet where he'd left the bucket. He opened the closet door and looked down at the bucket, dust pan covering the contents. As she followed Claire could see he was struggling with the problem.

"I'll have to tell him something. In fact I'm sure I will because I'll have to tell him what to test for. I won't tell him everything and whatever I do say you won't be included. You're right in wanting to keep it quiet. If it got out you saw this thing on one level you'd look like a nut. On another you just might be in danger. Me too for learning it second hand. Ether a government or an independent agency has become remarkably successful at doing something that I am certain they'd like to keep very secret."

On one of the shelves of the closet was a selection of gardening tools. He took a small hand trowel and knelt in front of the bucket

"What if it really is a cremated human body?" Claire asked.

Allan took the lid off the jar and a faint friendly smell of pickles drifted into the air.

"Then no matter what his faith in life as I see it that makes him my responsibility. I'm also caretaker for an old cemetery. It's not used any more. The youngest stones are fifty years old. The oldest is almost two hundred."

He took the dustpan off the bucket and set it aside. With infinitely more care than he had used when removing the matter from the wall rabbi Alan Rose began to use the trowel to transfer what was in the bucket to the jar.

"We won't be able to give him a name or a stone but we can give him a respectable burial. That is if you can call spending eternity in a pickle jar respectable."

CHAPTER 5

The lab was a secure facility that did medical research. Occasionally thanks to their specialized equipment they conducted certain tests connected to the identifying and treating of rare medical conditions and sometimes even did work for the police. Ordinarily people needed permission to get past the front door.

Alan Rose, carrying the pickle jar in a black cloth grocery bag simply paused so a security guard could pin a visitors badge on his jacket then continued on his way. He was there often, particularly at lunch time, and they knew him.

"Morning rabbi how's things?" asked the guard.

"Things are very well," Alan said. "He's in isn't he?"

"You know the boss," said the guard. "Every day like clockwork."

Moments later Dr. Samuel Bluestine head of the lab looked up from the work on the desk in front of him and smiled. Alan was standing in his open office door simply watching him. His friend always worked with his door open so he could be immediately accessible to his people. In spite of the myriad of distractions that echoed in from the surrounding office his concentration was absolute. Only when his eyes flicked up to look at a paper that sat at the edge of his desk did he see he had a guest.

"What're you sneaking around for?" he asked.

Alan smiled fondly at his longtime friend.

"I'm always fascinated by watching someone work at something they love," he said.

He entered the office and put the shopping bag with the pickle jar on his friend's desk. Sam's interest was immediately peeked. He set aside his pen.

"What's this?" he asked.

"I have brought you a puzzle. This is a substance that was stuck to the rear outside wall of a small synagogue down by the beaches," Alan explained.

"This would be your part time gig, morning prayers, the occasional wedding or bar mitzvah that place?" Sam asked.

"That's the spot. The stuff was stuck on the wall in the shape of a man with outstretched arms. How I have no idea."

Sam's brows raised in surprise. He tilted his head to one side in a way that told Alan that he definitely had his friend's full attention. No matter what the subject a slight tilt to the head was the first sign that this man was going to learn its secrets.

"So they wanted it to look a crucifix?" he asked.

"That's it exactly," Alan said. "The details of the figure were rough but that's what it looked like. The legs were together and the arms were outstretched and parallel. A tad more creative than spray paint but not nearly as permanent. Not permanent at all it just brushed off."

A question in his eyes Sam Bluestine circled the desk and took the pickle jar out of the bag. He turned the jar over in his hands studying the black substance through the clear glass. He shook his head slightly clearly at least temporarily at a loss.

He said, "You've got yourself a creative vandal Alan. Doesn't look like anything I recognize at first glance though."

"I know that's part of why I'm here," Alan said. "It was really strange. I took it off the wall with a dustpan and brush. The stuff just fell away."

Sam looked up at his friend. His curiosity had turned to concern.

"You breathe in any dust?" he asked.

"I must have, at least a little, but I feel OK," Alan said.

"That means it's not immediately toxic but that doesn't mean much," Dr. Samuel muttered.

Playing with the big jar in his hands Sam studied his friend closely. Alan shifted uncomfortably under this scrutiny. It was attention he had expected but that didn't make it any easier. There were very few people at this point in his life who knew him well enough to be able to tell when he was hiding something. There were his parents, his two sisters and this man.

"Alan, there's something here you're not telling me," he said finally.

"What do you mean?" Alan asked trying to stave off the inevitable.

"Don't give me that, you've got that, someone just told me a personal secret and it's bugging me, look in your eyes. I've seen it before." Sam said. "Hell I've caused it before."

Alan looked out the office window for a moment then back at his friend. Everything he had listened to that morning ran through his head like a bad dream. Only he knew when people were lying. Whatever the hidden truth about her experience was Claire Anderson had told him what she thought was the truth.

"You can't tell anyone," Alan said.

He cringed inwardly. He didn't sound like a grown man with an important secret he sounded like an eight year old who'd broken his mother's favorite vase.

"I mean it seriously Sammy this has to be between you me and God."

Dr. Samuel rolled his eyes in mild exasperation.

He said, "Shit, your bringing your boss into things. You almost never do that. This is serious. OK, you have my word."

Alan licked his lips and when he spoke he chose his words very carefully. He needed this man's help. Old friend or not if he wasn't convinced there might be a need for the tests he wanted performed those tests would not be done.

Reluctantly Alan said, "Sammy, I need to know if this stuff contains biological material of human origin."

Dr. Samuel Bluestine put the jar back on the desk with a firm thump. He crossed the room in three wide steps and closed his office door. When he turned back toward Alan his face now displayed open concern.

"What the hell have you gotten yourself into?" he demanded. "You better give me a good reason why you want this 'cause you just freaked the hell out of me."

Alan held up his hands as if defending himself from this sudden attack. He could tell his friend was more concerned than angry but that didn't make things any easier.

"Sammy I swear to you I personally am not actually involved in any-thing. I need to know if this is the remains of a man. I refuse to tell you why."

Sam sat in one of the two chairs in front of his desk and stared at the jar. He leaned his head in one hand elbow on the chair's arm.

"You can't tell me anymore or you won't tell me anymore," he said, pick-ing apart Alan's careful disclaimer. "You do know more, am I right?"

Alan sat in the other chair. He clasped his hands in his lap and leaned his elbows on the arms. In an attempt of casual normalcy he stretched his legs out and crossed his ankles. It didn't help to make things feel normal. That's because they weren't normal. When he finally spoke he kept his eyes on the floor.

"Sammy what little more I know you'd have problems believing. Even if I hadn't given my word I couldn't tell you. You're better off not knowing."

Dr. Samuel's mouth fell open as he read the very clear subtext under-neath his friend's statement. Alan knew where the understanding came from. He'd never known the exact nature of his friend's first research job as a freshly minted PHD. However the nature and scope of their abstract conver-sations involving morality had spoke volumes.

"Shit. That tells me a lot right there," Sam said. "This thing has covert action attached to it doesn't it?"

The scientist wiped his mouth with one hand and let his eyes drift over to the work on his desk. He wanted the problem to go away so he could climb back into his normal life. Alan was sorry that he was going to disappoint him. Some problems simply did not go away on their own.

"I owe you more than a couple Alan but this is a real stiff one," the scien-tist said finally.

"I know." Alan said simply.

Alan sat quietly and waited. He knew he was a smart man. You didn't even get into rabbinical school without a decent set of brains. This man sitting next to him was quiet simply a genius. But like many people with finely tuned brains he missed more than a bit in areas other than his specialty.

From his Bar Mitzvah on through his undergrad years the future doctor Samuel Bluestine had leaned on his best friend to drag him kicking and screaming through the humanities. The man could analyze a molecule in detail on two hours sleep. On the other hand you couldn't get him to understand a paragraph out of Shakespeare without help not even if you put a gun to his head.

Doctor Samuel thought for another long moment. Alan looked over at his friend and their eyes locked. In this way Alan saw denial of a challenge turn to acceptance.

"All right. I'll do the job."

Alan felt a large part of his inner tension relax.

"Is there any way you can do it without anyone else knowing?" he asked.

With a casual hand Sam waved away his friend's concerns.

"No problem. In fact if I wasn't sure I could do it without an audience I wouldn't be saying yes. Unless we get a rush job this place is empty on Sundays. I'll do all the work myself. I push pencils too much these days anyway. That paper work you so poetically admired me doing is nothing more scientific than the yearly budget. I could use some lab time."

"Good, it's a real long shot but the fewer people that know about this thing the safer I'll feel," Alan said.

He felt a shadow of his usual smile touch his face. The tension in the room had cut in half. Alan stood and looked down at his friend.

Sam looked up at him a half smile of his own lighting his face.

"You have to promise me if you can ever tell anyone what this is all about I get to know."

Alan held out a hand.

"Deal."

Samuel shook the hand and stood at the same time. When Alan let go of his friend's hand he set it gently on the pickle jar. His eyes became thoughtful.

"Sammy, I wouldn't have burdened you with this if I didn't think it was important," he said. "I need to know if this is something I need to bury respectably or if I can just toss it in the trash."

Sam looked from the jar to his friend. This scientifically rooted friend teased him constantly about his profession. At the same time Alan knew he had this man's respect.

"Taking care of lost soul's rabbi?" he asked.

Alan shrugged. It was a question that was an echo of the reason they had come together as boys at Hebrew school so many years ago. He was the child of scientifically minded parents who expected their son to be some sort of doctor or at the very least an engineer. His friend had been the only son of orthodox parents who had dreams of a rabbi for a son. They'd grown together understanding each other's pressures, and respecting each other's dreams.

"What can I say. It's part of the job."

*****

With the task of finding an answer to the mystery of the strange black ash given to Alan Rose, Claire found herself with little to distract from the business of organizing her holiday. She had attacked that business with an energetic combination of passionate data gathering and instant disinterest.

It was Friday afternoon, five days since she watched Alan Rose fill a pickle jar with respectful care. Maps and travel folders filled the house. They covered the dining room table, the kitchen table, the coffee table and just about every flat surface you could mention. She still didn't have a good idea of where she wanted to go but she defiantly had more than enough maps to get there.

Reflecting on the mess, Claire knew the real problem was something over which she had no control. She simply did not want to start on any kind of tour till she knew the answer to the riddle. Was the strange black dust the mortal remains of the man she had seen that night?

Trapped by her curiosity Claire took her frustrations out on her garden, pulling weeds and attacking dandelions with a passion. This was a good idea because gardening tended to take a back seat to housework, which took a back seat to her writing. This meant there was plenty of the nasty green spikey matter out there in the yard both front and back to fill the time.

Intent on pulling an extra spiky green thing out of the center of a rather limp cluster of flowers she was stopped by the ringing of the cordless phone sitting on her back deck. Half staggering to the deck she picked up her phone.

"Hello, weeds R us?" she said limply.

Jane Pendelton's voice came over the line and Claire slumped against the deck in dread anticipation. The woman sounded passionate. A passionate Jane Pendelton was a terrifying prospect.

"Claire please tell me you haven't made any reservations or done anything you can't cancel," she asked.

The feeling of imminent entrapment loomed large.

Claire said, "Not yet Jane. I've been taming my garden and reading travel folders. Why?"

"I've had a request from the publisher and it sounds like just what you need. It will mean a break and at the same time you'll be doing yourself some good," Jane said.

Claire felt a heavy lump hit the pit of her stomach. Jane was planning again. When Jane planned things happened. Usually that was a good thing but that didn't make it fun or relaxing.

Forgetting for a moment she had made a personal vow not to annoy this woman Claire gasped, "Oh lord Jane! Now what have you got me into?"

The voice on the phone was remarkably patient and reasonable. It was a voice that showed an understanding that caught Claire completely off guard.

"I haven't told them yes, but I did rather suggest I could talk you into playing ball. It's a sort of a mini lecture tour, three colleges. They had a last minute cancellation by the author that was supposed to come and speak and the publisher suggested you as a substitute. After all you're their new star."

Claire groaned and said, "But Jane, you know I'm no teacher. I'm not an academic at all. I'm self-taught. I'd sooner eat a dandelion than do research."

"Claire, dandelions are eatable. So are a great many other revolting things. I just sold a book that detailed the lot of them," Jane said. "When it's out I'll send you a copy."

Claire held her breath and counted to five before continuing. This woman might be acting like she understood her problem with this idea but she wasn't backing down. This was not a good thing.

Temper under control Claire said, "That's not my point. The most I could ever tell anyone would be keep writing till you get it right!"

"Then tell them that. It's really very simple. All you have to do is ease them into the notion that if they want to write for a living knowing how to dissect a chapter isn't quite the same as knowing how to write one. Anyway I've already sent you the information by courier. You read it and give me a buzz all right?"

Claire knew she was lost. She had become a "name" writer and "name" writers did lectures. Whether they wanted to do lectures or not was another thing altogether.

She said, "All right. I suppose it would give the trip a reason deter'. And if I screw up they won't offer me another one which is a good thing."

"Lets not worry about the future darling," Jane said cheerfully. "You know this means you'll be able to deduct most of your expenses. Isn't that a good idea?"

Claire had a sudden self-destructive urge to tell her agent exactly what kind of idea she thought this was but stopped. Jane Pendelton had changed her life and was infuriatingly right about just about everything. All she as the recipient of this good fortune had to do was concentrate on the "she's right" part and keep the infuriated part to herself.

"No comment," Claire said finally.

"Good. Now I promised I'd call them Monday and confirm so you take the weekend to think about it. I'll expect to hear from you Sunday night."

The dial tone filled her small yard with an incessant and slowly growing beep. Claire stared at the phone and quietly imagined all the colorful things one of her favorite characters would be saying. None of those things were polite and some of them would be in a language that didn't actually exist.

"One generally hangs up at this point."

Claire jumped at the sound of the male voice and turned the switch that silenced the beep. Alan Rose stood just inside the garden gate. In his right hand he held a cloth shopping bag with the pickle jar.

"You look like you've been stepped on slightly," he observed.

"I have, by my agent. She's a miracle worker in some ways. In others she tends to make me feel like a trailer park in Texas after bad storm," Claire admitted.

Alan looked around at the green disaster that was her back yard.

"I don't suppose she could make you feel like a gardener?" he asked.

"I'm not sure anything could manage that," Claire said. "I know practically speaking I probably should have got myself a nice fashionable condo so I could leave the landscaping to management but I just prefer houses."

Claire sat on her deck steps. Alan placed the pickle jar on the ground in front of the steps and sat down beside her. For a moment they sat side by side eyes on the bag in front of them.

"Bad news?" Alan asked, finally.

Feeling the usual effects of a conversation with Jane slip away Claire shook her head.

"No not at all. Actually a year or two ago I might have been thrilled. At this point though I'm just annoyed. She wants me to do a short speaking tour, three universities down south. The problem is I'm a doer not a speaker. I never even made it into university I'm self-taught. I don't really know if I could find the words to explain how I do what I do. I looked through a book once on how to write a novel. If I did even half of that crud that they say is invaluable I'd still be working on my first book."

Alan nodded his understanding and thought for a moment.

"One of my teachers early on told me teaching can be a bit daunting but it just takes practice. If you love your subject, no matter what the subject is, that goes a long way toward making you sound credible."

Claire found herself nodding her understanding. It was a fact she already knew but she'd never pictured herself on the teachers half of the equation.

"Okay that I already knew but what do I actually do?"

She asked. "Don't I need a lesson plan or something?"

"Well remember this is just a one shot lecture. Get the students to start talking then pick up on the parts they've got blatantly wrong and go from there. Talk to them."

Claire smiled and found herself relaxing considerably.

"Thanks, I think."

She put the phone on the deck and nodded toward the jar.

"So. What's the verdict?"

His face, pleasant and confident in the face of her personal crisis clouded over when reminded of their mutual puzzle.

"My friend wanted to do a lot of complicated testing that would take time. I told him I wanted an answer as soon as possible and would accept an educated guess," Alan said.

"And?" Claire prompted.

"By the way he's done his share of security level research so when I hinted at covert connections he agreed to not insist on to much information. According to the testing he did this is less than one sixteenth human matter. However there is biological matter. It's probably human and in much more than faint trace amounts. The rest is calcified brick dust, ordinary city dirt and a confusing bunch of chemicals he guessed to be weather sealant."

The latter fact distracted Claire slightly.

"Weather sealant?" she asked.

"The sort of thing you use to protect unpainted brick," Alan explained. "I better get a gallon of the stuff and reseal the wall or we'll have some expensive weathering that no one is going to understand."

Claire smothered a laugh at the combination of the strangely improbable and pragmatically ordinary. Alan caught her good humored reaction to his statement and they both shared a short tension relieving laugh.

"So your theory about maybe this just being loose skin cells and hair is right," Claire asked.

Alan sighed deeply and said, "It might me right. He also said the stuff was unusually charged, whatever that means. I'm afraid he's one of those passionate types. He's the head of a lab. When not coordinating other people's research he's busy with his own. When he gets worked up his ability to speak layman tends to suffer."

Claire sat staring at the unassuming shopping bag and its unusual contents for a long minute. The sun was bright and warm. The day was beautiful. At the same time they had a dark and gloomy problem.

"What do we do with it?" Claire asked.

"I'm going to bury it anyway," Alan said. "Unless you have any better ideas. We might know something. But in truth we really don't know if this man is alive or not. I was thinking on the way over here that its just possible the man really was killed and the rest of him was vaporized."

Claire grimaced at the picture.

"EUWWW...that's a cheery thought," she said.

"Sorry," Alan said. "It's a hangover from Torah study, kind of a reflex. After a while you can take any given situation or issue and look at it from at least ten different angles, and that's without trying."

Claire pulled her gardening gloves off and toyed with them, eyes on the jar.

"Burying it does sound like a good idea actually. Whether it's him or not if the stuff is charged with some kind of energy it might not be safe to simply scatter."

"My thoughts exactly," Alan said.

"OK let's go," Claire said. "Give me a minute to shut up the house. I'll meet you out front."

Claire tossed the gardening gloves to the deck then jumped to her feet. She picked up her phone and started for the back door. Alan jumped to his own feet and watched her go.

"You want to come?" he asked.

"Sure. I was here at the start of this nasty little tale I want to see it through. You know I almost hope that is whatever's left of him. He was clearly very afraid. He backed away from me like he didn't want me to get close enough to maybe get caught up in the nightmare."

Alan listened to this and nodded slightly.

"It's tragic but sometimes death really is the only freedom left," he said.

Claire glanced around at this her little patch of green. Here there was peace but beyond this quiet neighborhood the world could be a very different place.

"I think that's one of the reasons I write fantasy. In real life there are pitifully few happy endings. Anyway seeing this thing underground will make an ending of it for me. I'll go on my vacation with a clear conscious."

CHAPTER 6

Five minutes later Claire emerged from her front door to find Alan standing on the verandah. Locking the door she found herself feeling rather sheepish.

"Sorry I didn't invite you in but the place is a mess. Every once in a while I invite people over so I have to clean. For the past while though I've been working like an obsessed maniac on the rewrites for a screen play."

"No problem. My car's at the shule."

Claire pointed to her small red hatch back parked at the curb.

"Mine's just here. You had to pay for the gas that got you back and forth from your friends. Let's make this my trip."

Smiling at this logic Alan waved her ahead. Keys in hand Claire led the way to her car. Following his directions a fairly short city drive later Claire found herself looking for a parking place near a small cemetery surrounded by a high ironwork fence.

In the time period in which the cemetery had been created the area would have been open country. At this point the neighborhood consisted of densely populated working class housing, from small detached houses to high rise apartments. Finally Claire found a place to park the car two blocks away and they walked to the gate.

Alan said, "Geez the first time in two years I go walking with a pretty lady and we're going to a cemetery. There is undeniably something wrong with my life."

Claire smothered a giggle. There was defiantly something attractive about this man. Unfortunately there were other pragmatic matters that could not be ignored. It would be far better to get the facts out into the open.

"This is not a date it's a secret mission," she said. "Trust me I'd make a terrific friend but I'm really not your type. I'm a terrible house keeper, indifferent cook and I couldn't keep a kosher kitchen if my life depended on it."

"I've found the latter is a matter of desire and habit," Alan said. "My mother still doesn't keep kosher. As a compromise she keeps an extra nice stock of paper plates on hand just for me."

"I love it when families can find good solutions," Claire said.

"Yeah me too," said Alan.

"You'll have to admit though that it's a big jump from that to running an entire kitchen the proper way," Claire said. "I just couldn't manage it even if I wanted to. Alan my ex-husband made the mistake in assuming that all women are domestic in spite of how they seemed when they were single. It took him two years to figure out he was wrong. The kicker came a year later when we found out my ovaries were shooting blanks. Soon after that he fell in love with his secretary."

"I'm sorry. That's a couple of heavy shots," Alan said.

Claire smiled slightly at this sympathy. In some ways freedom from reproduction was a sad lost. In other ways it was an incredible liberation. Which she happened to feel depended on the day and the company.

"Oh it worked out all right. I have what I want and so does he. They live in the suburbs and just had a baby. I sent them a garden gnome for a house warming present. Anyway I'm babbling."

"Never underestimate the power of babbling," Alan said with a shadow of seriousness. "People say a great deal more when they babble. It tends to make counseling them much easier."

"I'm sure it does. I guess I'm trying to say I think you're a really nice guy and the sexiest rabbi I've ever met but...."

Alan smiled a little sadly as if it was the sort of statement he was used to hearing.

"All right, all right, I get the message," he said. "And I'd be the last one to sneer at an offer of friendship."

They stopped in front of a tall ironwork gate held closed by a strong chain and padlock. Claire held the jar as Alan locked the gate and led the way inside. Claire half expected the old gate to give a loud horror movie squeak. Instead it moved smoothly on well-oiled hinges. No doubt the work of the plot's energetic caretaker.

"Sign of the times this. You used to be able to leave the fence unlocked for anyone who wanted to come in and do rubbings on the older stones or simply sit under a tree and think. Now its only safe to leave it open on the Sabbath and for holidays. Even then we get problems."

Claire pulled the gate closed and draped the chain in a way that made it look to the casual observer as if it were still locked. Claire looked around at the island of silence they had just entered then out at the drab reality of the world that surrounded them. Both neighborhood as a whole and cemetery were cramped and overcrowded. In here however there was a sense of time and rest the outside world could never manage.

"For some people being alive is not necessarily a recommendation," she said. "You sure your friend wont blab about this?"

Alan used another key on his key ring to unlock the door of a small tool shed. He reached in and took out a gardening shovel.

He said, "No problem there. I told him just enough to impress on him the possible danger of anyone finding out he knew about this, and like I said he owes me. This is the first time I've had reason to call him on the debt."

"Must be one heck of a debt," Claire said.

"It's kind of long and complicated. His parents are very religious but he could care less. If it weren't for me tutoring him incessantly he'd never have been able to do his bar-mitzvah."

Alan stood with the shovel for a moment surveying the headstone packed yard. He nodded toward a huge old tree standing in the middle of the space and began to lead the way. Walking carefully and trying as best they could to avoid stepping on the graves themselves they threaded their way toward their goal.

"Is he a lot younger than you?" Claire asked.

"Actually he's four years older," Alan said. "When we met he was hanging around with my older sister."

"You must have been a real wiz kid," Claire observed.

"That's where the debt starts adding up. You see he's something of a genius in the math's and sciences; I maxed out on the humanities, languages, History, Religion. You can get through university with almost no maths or sciences, but even a science major has to take English. Heck he had problems in high school. I fully expect him to grab a Nobel Prize someday and I have given notice I better get a thank-you. When did you start writing?"

Claire thought for a moment and shrugged. It was a question that had an answer that was somewhat less than straightforward.

"I was born writing. Before I could actually string sentences together on paper I drew pictures in sequence and invented stories in my head for them. I have that kind of mind, it takes in data and then twist's it around and spits out plot. It would do it even if I didn't write. The problem is I spell horribly. I didn't really have a chance to get anywhere with the writing till affordable home computers with spell and grammar check came on the market."

They reached the tree and Alan studied the ground carefully. Hugging the pickle jar in its bag Claire stood a little out of the way watching. She had an idea that besides carpentry he had done more than his share of heavy digging.

"Life's like that," Alan said. "Sometimes a persons vocation is born with them. It's their job to find what it is then solve whatever problem that goes along with becoming what they already are."

There was a large circle of bare earth around the tree which was broken by thick roots. Alan began to loosen the earth closest to the tree gradually working his way around the tree and away from the trunk in several concentric circles. When most of the bare earth had been turned over he chose a spot in between two large branching roots and began to dig down.

As he dung eyes were distant. Claire guessed that distance was being filled with a memory, or perhaps more than one. It looked very much like a maze of memories dredged up by their talking about his friend her profession and life in general.

"You know my problem what's yours?" she asked.

"My problem will always be with me, and I've yet to find any real solution. It's rather poetic really. You know how I told you my friend's parents were religious?"

"Yup."

"They would have given anything to have a rabbi for a son. They encouraged me incredibly. My parents on the other hand as I said before don't even keep kosher and would have much preferred a scientist. My dad's always wanting me to go to teachers college so I can get a real job. I keep telling him, "Dad I have a real job." but he just doesn't get the message."

When the hole he was digging got to be just slightly more than two feet deep Alan took the jar, still wrapped in the cloth bag, and placed it on its side on the cool earth. He stood closed his eyes and Claire could see his lips moving in some silent prayer. When he finished the whispered missive he knelt and began pushing the soil over the jar by hand. Claire bent to help and soon the hole was full and the extra soil displaced by the bottle spread so that it simply looked as if a gardener had dug up the space around the tree to allow the roots to breath.

Claire sat back on her heels and studied Alan Rose who also relaxed back taking a seat on the grass.

"Life's a strange joke sometimes," she said. "A writer that can't spell and a rabbi with secular parents."

"Yeah we're a real odd couple," Alan said.

He looked out at the small field full of headstones. The dark shadow of the memories had gone. In their place was a satisfied man who knew who he was and his place in the world.

"The real joke is there are people that think they can avoid the punch line. They waste their lives doing what other people want them to do instead of what their passion dictates. Life is far too short to spend it avoiding your passion because there are parts of it that are less than practical."

They looked around at the silent stones feeling the stillness that seemed full of decade's dead souls. Claire was pulled away from this contemplation by a hollow feeling about the waistline. She looked at her watch and found it was twenty minutes to one.

Will you look at the time. It's almost past lunch."

Claire climbed to her feet and dusted off both hands and jeans.

"It's my turn to provide the food I think," she said. "Buy you a bagel rabbi?"

Following her example Alan Rose also climbed to his feet and dusted off his hands. He picked up the shovel and started toward the shed.

"Throw in some cream cheese and a cup of coffee Miss Anderson, and you got yourself a deal."

CHAPTER 7

If there was ever one thing that history could teach the imprisoned it was there were very few places that were completely escape proof. The prisoner simply needed luck, strength and a lot of patience. David St. John had patience and strength. Finishing the job of prying up the floor boards to his shed sized prison he hoped fervently he would rate some good luck to make up for the bad that had brought him to this hellish place.

Trying hard not to impale himself on any exposed splinter or nail John pushed himself through the narrow space he had spent two weeks making. Like many buildings in this place the shed was set up on cinder blocks to reduce the wood rot being set directly on the ground would produce. This also gave him a chance to wait in sheltered secrecy as he judged his surroundings. He'd gotten this far several times and then retreated. This looked like the golden moment.

Not a soul could be seen with the exception of a single guard at the gate who sat in a chair that leaned against a post. His gentle snores drifted through the night. It was time to go but it wouldn't be easy. His wrists were held in front of him by a set of handcuffs. His ankles were manacled with a three-foot length of chain between. It was enough for walking but not enough for any kind of respectable speed.

David slipped out from under the shed and hobbled directly toward the perimeter fence that surrounded the compound. Moving as quickly as possible he followed it searching desperately for a weakness, something that would prevent him from having to concede failure and climb back into his wooden cell once more.

He found his chance in the best possible place. He had trailed the fence behind one of the bigger buildings. The wire fencing was no looser here but he was out if sight of the guard and there was a shovel leaning against the building. David used the shovel to pry up the fencing just enough to let him slip underneath the wire.

Heart thumping in his chest hard enough to make him dizzy he stood on the other side of the fence. Reminding himself this wasn't freedom just a different kind of danger he turned and began to run.

*****

David St. John hobbled through the pre-dawn wood. He moved carefully but with an unrelenting slow motion effort born of desperation. In spite of the cool night air beads of sweat on his forehead and back spoke of his intense effort.

He was running for his life at the speed of a slow tired jog and the nearest town was twenty miles away. Pushing despair from his mind he kept moving. Stealth would have to substitute for speed. It was all he had.

The short chain between his ankles was forcing him to divide his attention between trying to decide which direction he should go and avoiding the rocks sticks and other underbrush that tried to reach out grab the restraints and send him falling to the ground. He'd fallen more than once collecting several bloody scrapes in the process. What was worse the falls had slowed him down.

The wood was deathly silent but for the constant harsh rasping of his breath and the sound of his feet hitting the ground. Then it wasn't silent. He froze and listened. Men were moving in the wood. They were hunters, hunting him!

He stopped then crouched down and listened carefully trying to judge where these followers were. The sound picture that came to him made depressing news. They were scattered behind him, moving patiently through the trees in his direction.

Moving carefully from tree to tree he continued in the same direction he had been going, roughly parallel to the narrow private drive that ran out of this small valley to the world. If he could make the highway this road ran off of he had a chance.

His speed began to usurp care. He fell, rose and ran again. He slipped down a muddy bank and crossed an ice cold stream slipping and sliding on water smooth stones.

Lying on the streams opposite bank he listened. They were getting closer and what was worse the sounds of pursuit were now in front of him. He was surrounded. Hope dyeing he looked for a place to hide.

The sound of the chase became huge. Shadow men came toward him through the pre-dawn gloom. He tried for one last burst of speed but the chain at his ankles hooked on a dead branch and he fell full out onto a blanket of leaves and dead pine needles!

Against his will he gave a sob of deep sorrow. How far had he gotten, one mile, two? What would this little fresh air jog cost him?

Men surround him and pulled him to his knees. Trembling with exhaustion he slowly looked up at the man who followed these others.

They called him Master. His face was tanned and lined like an outdoorsman. He had a short head of thick white hair. He couldn't be any younger than seventy but he still had the strong body of an active man twenty or thirty years his junior. When he spoke his words were delivered with the authority of a sermon.

"David St. John, when a man learns of Gods fate for him he must submit. God's will is all supreme," he intoned.

A gut wrenching feeling of anger welled up inside David at this statement.

"You lunatic!" he yelled. "God has nothing to do with any of this!"

The younger men stiffened at this defiant exclamation. The old man simply shook his head sadly.

"It is clear the sacrifice is one with the sin of pride."

The old man pointed to a tree. One of the lower branches had fallen off so that there was a two-foot long hook at a place just taller than the comfortable reach of a man.

David stared at the small stump of a branch at a total loss. Strong hands grabbed his arms and lifted him up. Resisting limply David found he had to save most of what strength of will that he had left to stop himself from asking what they were going to do.

They forced his wrists above his head then lifted him up and hooked him on the branch. When they let go he found his feet were just able to reach the ground and save himself from the horror of simply hanging from the restraints at his wrists. What horror they were going to replace it with he didn't want to know but he knew it wouldn't be long in coming.

"The Blessed one must be cleansed," declared the Master.

David looked over his shoulder as far as he could turn. He saw the eager faces of men lit by the sun of the new day and flush from the excitement of the chase. They were eager for something else too and when the sound of a whip cut the air David knew what that something was.

"We will begin that cleansing now!"

*****

David St. John lay on the thin mattress in the dark box of a prison he had tried so hard to escape. He lay on his stomach gripping the mettle framework of the bed as the entire shed vibrated with the concussion of hammers.

They were underneath the small shed reinforcing the floor with metal supporting beams. Even if he managed to get a board up again he would be faced with a sub floor of iron bars. Unless his world changed drastically escape was now impossible.

The banging stopped. The men gathered their tools and extra materials then left. David thanked whatever God was welcome to listen for the mercy of stillness that lessened the pain coming from his back. Now it was just a steady throb.

The Master had done his job well. He hadn't broken the skin, which would have invited a battle with infection. He had simply raised a thatch pattern of crisscrossed welts that made every movement agony. Not that this wooden box of a prison offered many options for movement.

David's mind drifted back to the day he had been taken. He had been standing on one of the high hills on the edge of this property. He'd seen little of consequence and had been about to leave.

"You're trespassing mister."

It was the old man with ten of his acolytes. They'd come up behind him silent as shadows. He'd been startled but had caught himself quickly and pulled out his ID wallet.

"David St. John, FBI, I monitor cults and other groups that set up isolated fenced in compounds," he said.

The Master studied his identification intently then gave it back. The old man had been cool and self-confident, his followers more than a touch indignant.

One spoke up as he put away his identification, "We got a right to build a place of our own."

"I never said you didn't. Technically I'm not even on your land. Your land begins about ten feet that way. I looked it up in the hall of records so I wouldn't be stepping on your toes."

The younger men had bristled at this statement. The Master had smiled slightly. Taking the smile as a sign of at least partial understanding David had decided complete business like honesty was the best approach.

"Look lets be honest here. You boys have to know the government is interested in groups like yours. We don't want to interfere in religion we just want to make sure whoever is here is here by choice. We also want to make sure you're not funding your operation by doing anything illegal like for instance gun or drug smuggling. Groups such as yours have been known to do that."

The old man had given a sage like nod of agreement.

"There are those that sin in the name of God. I am leader here. Will you enter and see for yourself this place is nothing but a gathering of the faithful?"

He'd accepted the invitation and shouldered his backpack and walked beside the old man till they had entered the compound. There in the center the man had waved his follower's forward. It had cost them some bumps and bruises and at least one broken arm but they'd gotten him stripped and face down in the dirt. Where the old man had examined his tattoo intently.

"The mark of old faith," he said.

"My family's Irish you son-of-a-bitch! It's just an old Irish pattern."

"God marks some chosen. Others he causes them to mark themselves."

Totally taken aback he'd struggled to look up at the old man that seemed to be in a religious swoon. For the first time in his life he felt totally helpless and completely confused.

"What is this all about? You know who I am! You didn't have to let me in here! What the hell is this all about?"

"We will not have to risk the experiment on one of our faithful. God has sent this chosen one to be our sacrifice as he did when he sent the ram to be a substitute for Isaac's only son."

He'd spent the rest of that day firmly bound and under a silent guard. That night they had done the experiment for the first time. After that first horror they had shut him up in here.

It had a bed a chemical toilet and a hole cut in the door big enough for a bowl to be put through. The hole, looking much like a cat door, was covered on the outside with an opaque flap. The flash of brightness whenever someone brought him food was the only bit of natural sun he had seen in weeks.

"Blessed one?"

It was the voice of a young woman. One of several who had the job of bringing him his food. He struggled to find his voice. In spite of his pain he wanted to do what he'd been doing since the beginning talk and force them to if only for a moment acknowledge that he was a man.

"My name is David," he said finally.

He wasn't even sure he'd said it loud enough to be heard. When she spoke he knew he had.

"We're not supposed to call you that," she said.

David sighed deeply. He was the blessed one, the one who would be the first to see god while still alive. He knew their whole liturgy by heart. It sickened him.

"What do you want?" he asked.

The soft voice continued and for the first time it had some personality. She was speaking as a person not simply one of the group.

"I know we're not supposed to use them it's against gods will, but my pa used to whup me like that sometimes. Well, not quite like that but real hard."

A thin female hand slipped through the flap in the door delivering a large mug. David smelled chicken broth.

"There's aspirin in the soup. I stirred it so they dissolved. I only had four in my purse. I don't think it will do a lot but it was all I had."

Slipping off the bed David moved toward the smell half crawling the short distance and crouching by the door. He cupped his hands around the mug on the floor breathing in the aroma and feeling its comforting warmth.

"Thank you. What's your name?"

"Sally-May"

"Do you ever leave the compound Sally-May?" he asked. "Can you please tell someone I'm here. Anyone. This thing they're doing to me. It's going to kill me. It doesn't have anything to do with religion Sally-May its just torture and it's pointless."

He heard her sit on the step just outside the door. She was listening. For the first time since he had tried talking to these faceless female voices one of them was listening. Like the run through the wood this was another chance that he had to take.

He said, "Sally, the chief of campus police at the college in town knows I was in the area. If you call his office anonymously he'll know what to do. You won't have to give your name. You won't get in trouble. The master will never know it was you."

He slumped against the door and imagined he could feel the young woman sitting so close, struggling with her loyalties. He knew a lot about girls like this. They were rootless, lost, that was why the clung to leaders like the Master. He gave them what they in most cases never had, certainty and a place to belong.

"The master wouldn't like that. I don't think I ought to talk to you anymore."

David heard Sally-May get up from the step and hurry away. Shaking his head against her flight into dogma he picked up the mug. His hands and arms trembled with the effort and for once he welcomed the unforgiving blackness. He drank the soup in small sips, willing his stomach to hold in the liquid long enough to at least absorb the painkiller. At the same time praying that four aspirin were strong enough to take the edge off his pain.

He had more prayers far less likely to succeed. He prayed desperately that sometime soon this basically good girl would find the strength to do the right thing. Like most cult members in this and others she was a good girl that understood right and wrong. It was only the greater good preached by the Master that prevented her from acting. For some reason this girl and the others like her desperately wanted to get to heaven. They thought they could get there while still alive.

David closed his eyes and in his mind he saw the face of that unnamed woman standing in the center of the street. His senses when he traveled were confused and distorted. Once he had simply fallen to the ground blind and deaf and dumb. He'd lain there motionless until he had felt the power begin to pull him back.

He hadn't been able to hear the woman very well and he couldn't speak. But he remembered her face and he remembered her clear desire to help. It had been an image that he held fast in his mind.

She had wanted to help. There was no way she would ever be able to but just knowing that desire existed in the world calmed his soul and helped him hope this girl who actually could help would act.

Hanging onto this mental picture David St. John slowly downed his lunch. He slipped his hands through the door putting the mug outside on the top step and sat leaning against the locked door for a long time listening to the free world that revolved around his small prison. Feeling exhaustion overtake his pain he crawled back to his bed for a long dreamless sleep.

CHAPTER 8

The information package from Jane Pendelton arrived the next morning in the hands of a fresh-faced young courier who looked like he recognized her from the small photograph on the rear flap of her book. Claire ignored the look signed the courier slip and closed her front door.

Being recognized like this was a curious experience she had begun to encounter since the book had launched six months previously and generally enjoyed. This time all she could think of was the ordeal the package she was signing for represented.

Fortified with a box of chocolate chip cookies she sat down to read what the envelope contained and slowly began to relax. By the time she finished reading the contents she was cautiously optimistic that this could actually be an enjoyable experience.

She reached for the phone and dialed the agent's number. The voice on the other end of the phone was warm but eternally business like. It was a voice Claire expected. Jane never turned on the charm unless it was needed.

"Jane Pendelton here."

"Ok Jane I'll do the tour," Claire said.

The tone of voice turned from all business to cat with a craw full of canary. Claire had to fight to keep from laughing.

"Fabulous darling you'll have balls of fun I know it!"

Claire rolled her eyes at the satisfied sound in the agent's voice. She hated feeling predictable at the same time the ability to read people was this woman's stock in trade. You couldn't blame someone for simply being who they were.

"If you say so Jane. I'm just glad the thing came up at the last minute. I'd hate to have too long to prepare. I get terrible stage fright you know."

"Get used to it darling I told you when I took you on. You are going to be a star. There's no two ways about it."

Claire finished the conversation quickly sensing that Jane had work she was eager to return to then got off the phone and went to pack.

The tour consisted of three small colleges in three different southern states. Each school was located in a small town. This would be an excursion into the world of small town America. For a big town Canadian girl this fact alone qualified the trip as a great adventure. Small town anywhere was a concept with which she simply had no experience.

The first of these lecturer/teaching adventures was only a week away. Claire pushed her travel plans into over-drive and on the appropriate day she got in the car and began to drive south.

The program schedules were as identical. First there was a "meet the author" social event on a Sunday evening. This event would be attended by teachers and an assorted selection of hand-picked students.

The next day there were classes and other events scheduled depending on what sort of English program that particular college offered. After that baring accepting any other appointments or invitations she would have the rest of the week to move on to the next school.

The first social evening pointed out small holes in the apparent simplicity of this plan. The difference between drinks and mixing as written in a travel schedule and actually doing it was immediately apparent.

As a representative of the world of working writers they saw in her a valuable source of information. It was a part she was willing to play knowing from personal experience how even a little practical advice would have prevented some time wasting mistakes. However, explaining the world of professional writing to well-educated but in many instances idealistic academics was not easy.

"Miss Anderson I realize fantasy fiction is paying the bills but I was wondering if you were working on some important, that is, a more socially significant project."

The questioner was in his late sixties with a round face and short thinning gray hair. Claire opened her mouth to speak and found that she had absolutely nothing diplomatic to say to this intensely opinionated man. Instead she gave the man the carefully stated but unvarnished truth.

"It's a curious western chauvinism that downgrades fantasy and science fiction. In Japan they consider the genre's equal and reward good writing regardless. As for the money aspect I find owning my own home free and clear very significant. People find my work entertaining. These are people who have the power to do me personally some good. They feel I have the chance to develop a wide audience and I like to think they're right. I find that significant as well."

Glancing around at the people who were witnessing this encounter Claire could see that she had scored a point. Eyes just a little wide with clearly felt disbelief he battled on.

"Do you truly want that to be your epitaph?" he asked. "She was entertaining."

There was a sincere tone to the man's pronouncement that Claire found close to hilarious. Her energetic laughter caused the professors brows to rise in silent surprise.

In answer to this she said, "You know, I don't think I'd mind that a bit. People who write socially significant work are enviably ignored in their time, frequently by authorities such as yourself. They end up dyeing young and poor. I'm too old to die young so I'll settle for being comfortably middle class and entertaining."

The comment brought amused smiles and some laughter from the surrounding crowd. The professor rolled his eyes slightly, smiled politely and excused himself. She hadn't won him over and likely never would. But she had defended her view well and the crowd approved.

The rest of the evening went smoothly. At ten o'clock she was driven to her motel. Her driver was the same senior student who had picked her up three hours before.

When he picked her up he had greeted her politely and driven without comment. This time he talked non-stop about a book he wanted to write but was not sure he could. Two drinks past her usual limit Claire listened with relative tolerance, which slowly blended into annoyance.

He pulled into the parking lot of the motel where she was staying and parked in front of the main entrance. Claire unbuckled her seat belt then turned and she fixed him with as firm a gaze as she was capable.

"Write the damn thing or don't. If you talk the subject to death or worse spend twenty years on the outline it will never get written and you will never know if you could have succeeded. That's my first and last word on the subject for the evening."

He opened his mouth as if to speak but she continued before he had a chance.

"If you have some practical questions to ask me save them for class. At this point I am much too drunk to make any sense of anything. Good night!"

Claire left the car in one smooth move and slammed the door with a flourish. Tottering only slightly and mentally congratulating herself for the fact she left him without looking back.

Set just outside the town limits the two story motel was lined on one side by farmers' fields and on the other by a meadow which stretched out to a line of trees. Feeling the effects of the wine even stronger now that she was out in the fresh air Claire climbed the steps to the balcony running around the second floor and strolled along to her room. Key in hand she paused in front of her door and looked out at the moonlit meadow breathing in the scents of the night.

An electric crackle echoed in the cool night air. Claire looked up at the star filled sky and pouted. There was something about the sound that was familiar. She looked back at the rooms and at the lights that illuminated the parking lot. It could not be lightning and there was no sign of problems with the electricity.

Then he was there. Like a living crucifix his arms were stretched out with his hands balled into fists. His legs were together with his feet hovering a foot above the pavement of the parking lot. His body was arched as if in pain and his mouth open in a silent scream. After a full second he fell to the ground.

Frozen in place Claire looked down on the man. Her shocked mind quickly took in slight differences from her first vision. He was still nude. This time however instead of just lines of chafing at his wrists and ankles there were several bruises and a mass of welts on his back as if from a whip. Looking at him crumpled on the ground Claire felt a surge of impotent pity.

"This is really happening isn't it?"

The question was only whispered but he looked up at her as if the words had been yelled. He pushed himself to his feet and stood wavering uncertainly as if a light breeze might have the power to bowl him over. She spoke again keeping her voice soft since it was clear he didn't need her to yell and neither one of them wanted company from the other guests of the motel.

"Look, you remember me from before don't you?" she asked. "I want to help. Let me help you!"

Slowly he looked around at his surroundings, moving his whole body instead of just his head. His every movement advertised the fact that he was intensely stiff and sore. His leg muscles trembled badly, as if simply standing was a huge effort. Finally his arresting blue eyes found her. He stood looking up, arms hanging limp.

"Look, it doesn't take a genius to guess you're a prisoner," she said softly. "Help me help you. Give me some kind of sign. Who has you? Is it the government?"

He shook his head. His eyes became unfocused as if he were trying to think and the effort was almost past his ability. Claire took a step toward the closest set of stairs. Seeing this he panicked, holding up his hands and shaking his head in an obvious display that told her to stay where she was.

"All right, all right, I get the idea," she said. "It might dangerous to be too close to you when they pull you back."

He nodded then half-staggering he backed away from her, bumping into a large planter full of flowers. He looked at the space between two rows of flowers for a long moment then leaned over the planter and Claire could see his hand moving, smoothing the soil. He appeared to write something with a stick, then smooth the earth flat and write again. It almost seemed as if he could not remember how to spell what he wanted to say.

"Just keep it phonetic kid I'll understand," she said.

The man looked up, the gratitude in his eyes brought a lump to Claire's throat. There was something else as well, a warmth and a strength Claire had never seen. There was a strength in this man that existed in spite of his pain, in spite of his fear. Looking up at her like this he seemed like a battered and long imprisoned knight errant.

Startling them both and breaking the silent connection that had brought them strangely together the lights of a car pulled into the lot. He broke away and ran off into the meadow toward the row of trees.

Seeing more danger than discovery in this unwelcome interruption Claire bolted toward the nearest stairs. A man and woman got out of the car to watch astonished as the naked man fled. They were both understandably shocked.

"Who the hell is that?" asked the man.

Claire ran up to the car. In the process she did her best to put herself between the newcomers and the planter. They had to be distracted, stopped before they did the most natural thing and tried to track this strange man down.

"That is just so crazy," she said. "I was going to my room when I noticed him in the parking lot. I think he's in some kind of trouble."

The man looked from her to the fleeing figure. His eyes narrowed in suspicion.

"Yeah I'll bet. You sure he's not running away from you?" he asked.

Claire rolled her eyes at this vague accusation and said, "Don't be silly. Do I look like the sort of person any grown man would run away from?"

The faint figure of the running man disappeared into the wall of trees. An electric crackle rent the air. Claire's shoulders slumped knowing that he had yet again vanished.

"Is that lightning?" said the woman. "Strange. There's not a cloud in the sky."

With her companions distracted by the sound Claire took a moment and looked down at the words written in the soil of the planter. She then looked up at her unwelcome audience. She did not want these people to know any more than they did already, that meant the next move had to be managed very carefully.

"I was just getting back from a thing at the college in town when I noticed him standing in the lot. Funny thing was he didn't seem drunk or anything. I wonder why he's in the buff?"

The planter was large almost bench height. It took very little acting for Claire to totter slightly and drop bottom down onto the desperately scribbled word. It messed her good dress but it also eliminated the evidence.

"You okay?" asked the man.

Claire looked over to find the man had a phone in his hand. He seemed to be waiting for someone to answer his call. It no longer mattered who he called or told. The police could comb the wood lot they wanted to and still find nothing.

"I had a little too much to drink this evening and I'm not thinking very clearly. Or walking to well come to think of it," she said. "Who are you phoning?"

"My editor," he said. "I write for the National Star. This sort of thing is right up our alley."

Claire smiled at the eager sound in the man's voice. Brushing potting soil off her dress she started back toward the steps up to her room.

"Mazeltov I'm happy for you," she muttered.

"Hang on, don't you want your name in the paper?" he asked.

Claire giggled shook her head and kept walking.

"Nope. Not in yours anyway," she said talking over her shoulder. "What I want is a dark room and a soft bed. I feel just a little unwell."

Claire walked up the stairs getting to the door just as the man's companion spoke up indignantly.

"Bobby! I thought you were on vacation!" she said.

Feeling very drunk and very tired Claire laughed softly to herself as she wrestled with the room key and opened her door. Not too long ago she'd said the same thing to her then husband. It was interesting to note some things were universal.

"It'll only take a few minutes. Hell Annie you saw it yourself the guy was really strange. We should probably phone the cops while we're at it," said the writer.

"The police! Oh no you don't!" she declared. "I am not spending my holiday in a police station. If some lunatic wants to run around in the nude that's up to him. He's not hurting anyone."

The man's tone of voice as he answered this statement raised Claire's opinion of him several notches. Maybe he did write for a tabloid, but he was also a caring human, capable of worrying about a stranger.

He said, "But Annie story aside he might really be in trouble. He looked kind of battered."

"What if he did," she said reluctantly. "If he wanted our help he would have stayed and let us help him."

Claire closed and locked her door on the budding argument. The woman had a point but it was a point that clearly showed she was not as keen an observer as her tabloid writer escort. Claire stretched out on her bed in the darkened room. Grabbing for the pencil and pad on the bed side table she wrote three words then dropped the pen and paper back beside the phone. She then kicked off her shoes and fell sound asleep.

CHAPTER 9

Monday evening Hebrew study class was assembled. Alan Rose sat at his desk in one corner of his living room and watched the three boys who sat at his small dining room table. They were writing intently, filling the room with the blanketing feel of deep concentration. The telephone rang, shattering feeling of concentration filled quiet. Both students and teacher jumped. Enjoying their teacher's discomfort in a way that distracted them from their own reaction the boys burst out laughing.

"That's enough of that please," Alan said.

Alan lifted the receiver silencing the sound. Staring the laughing boys silent and back to work Alan then turned his attention to the phone in his hand.

"Hello?"

"Alan it's me Claire, am I interrupting anything?"

Alan smiled into the phone. He glanced back at the boys to see that the veil of total concentration had truly been shattered. They were still working that was clear, but at least half their attention was covertly fixed in his direction.

I have some students here I'm tutoring. They're doing a sample test right now so I can talk," he said. "How's your tour going?"

"I've finished the first school and getting ready to move on to the next. It's going much better than I thought it would. The social evening with the teachers and seniors was interesting in a way. The sessions with the students were kind of fun. That's not why I phoned. I thought you'd like to know that our vanishing friend is still in the land of the living."

Alan almost fell out of his chair in surprise. It was something he would never have imagined.

"What did you say?" he asked.

"I saw him again," she said. "He appeared Sunday night in the parking lot of my hotel of all things."

Desperately wishing his young audience was anywhere else Alan turned toward his desk and leaned his head in one hand. When he spoke it was with a quiet concern.

"There must be something we can do about this. I wonder if the FBI has an anonymous tip line?" he pondered.

At the table the boys exchanged looks of open-eyed curiosity. One of them spoke up.

"They've got a web site," he said.

Alan glanced over at the boy who smiled shyly, knowing he wasn't supposed to have over heard.

"Well, they do," he said.

"Hang on Claire, the walls here have ears and one set of those ears has said the FBI has a web site," Alan said into the phone.

The young student at the table raised his voice so he could be heard on the phone.

"The CIA does too," this boy offered. "It's neat."

Claire laughed as Alan relayed this second bit of information and said; "I think we can leave the CIA out of this and stick with the FBI. I'll send them an anonymous e-mail. I don't know if it will do any good but something must be done and soon. He looked pretty battered this time Alan. He's been fighting his captors. I just wish I could do more. Every time I close my eyes I see him standing there right in front of me and I get this sick feeling in the pit of my stomach."

Vividly aware of the sharp minds that were taking in every nuance of what they could see and hear of this conversation Alan struggled to choose his words carefully. When he spoke he kept his voice even, his tone light. Freelance bar-mitzvah tutors did not talk of matters of life and death.

"We have to work with what we're given Claire. If we can't solve this problem in time perhaps we can prevent another problem from occurring," he said.

The line was quiet for a moment as Claire though over what Alan had said. It didn't take long for her to put her understanding into words.

"You mean if they kill this man maybe they'll keep on experimenting with another victim," she said.

"My thoughts exactly," Alan answered.

"Okay that's what I'll do. Thank your helpful set of ears for me will you?"

"All right. I'll also thank him to not be such a nosy parker and pay attention to his Hebrew."

He was about to hang up when Claire said something else.

"Do the words "the Philadelphia experiment" mean anything to you?" she asked.

Alan's mouth hung open for a moment as he searched his memory. The words struck a chord but the memory was uncertain and its meaning unclear.

"I, I think it's a movie title," he said. "Why?"

"He wrote it in the soil of a planter," she said. "It took a lot of effort so it has to be important. I'm moving on to the second school tomorrow morning. When I get there I'm going to take some time and do a web search and see if I can come up with anything."

The faint memory of a picture of a ship laying on its side in the middle of the desert drifted through the back of Allan's mind. He had seen it recently he was sure.

"Want me to see if I'm right about the movie?" he offered.

"Sounds good," she said. "I'll call you in a day or so."

Alan Rose hung up the phone and eyed his students.

"No the rabbi is not into something wild and dangerous. Eyes down if you please."

*****

It took Claire most of Tuesday to drive to the next town. She located the hotel and checked in. Taking advantage of the establishment's wireless internet she searched the web for something called The Philadelphia Experiment. The result was considerably more than she expected.

After an hour's worth of reading she chose a web service that provided free e-mail. She then created an e-mail name with false personal information then looked for and found the FBI's web site. The final step was to write a long and very detailed e-mail. They would be able to trace the letter back to this mailbox but as she had no intention of using it more than once they would never be able to trace it back to her.

"I am not going to tell you my real name. But I urge you to take this message seriously. I have seen something twice and you must investigate it. Unless I am very wrong a man's life is in danger."

She went on to detail her two visions. In the process of her description she was careful to explain she had been in the second location simply because like thousands of other travelers she was driving south to Orlando for a theme park holiday and had stopped for the night.

"I understand fully that you might think me a simple crackpot. If you wish confirmation you might contact the office of the tabloid newspaper The National Star and ask them if one of their reporters also on vacation phoned in a story about a naked man that ran off into a wood and disappeared."

She sent the e-mail and turned her computer off. Lying in the bed with the television playing she closed her eyes and saw him; deep pleading blue eyes, prominent cheekbones. It was a face she could fall in love with. It was a face she would probably never see again.

*****

The lecture hall was in the form of an amphitheater with curved rows of seats on many levels. It was packed full of students all paying strict attention to the open space in front of them which held only a chalk board on the wall, a speaker's podium and a slightly nervous writer.

"Do you ever worry that any of your plots might be demonically inspired?"

The young man who sat in the center of the class had asked several questions all with religious themes. Claire sighed deeply. At home she would have countered this question with a flippant "hell no." That would not work

74

here. This was the American south, Christian fundamentalist country frequently referred to as the Bible belt. It was politic to take these kinds of questions with the same seriousness with which they were asked.

"You can't be afraid of your own mind if you're going to write. Evil is in the eye of the beholder. If you're going to write and really come up with something original you have to let your imagination drift. You can't do that if you try and edit every thought before it even becomes a thought."

The teacher, one eye on the clock on the wall, stood and came to the center of the stage.

"Well this has been a very informative session Ms. Anderson and I think I speak for the whole English program when I thank you very much for coming."

The large group applauded warmly, then slowly scattered. Some left the hall, some gathered in groups talking about the class, some came down the steps toward her, still wanting to talk. The very religious young man was first in this last group.

"I think you're the only person who ever gave me a good answer to that question," he said.

"I always wanted to be the first at something," Claire said.

Now that he was closer Claire noticed a four-inch long cross hanging around his neck on a chain. It looked as if it were made of polished iron or some other hard wearing metal. On each end of the cross bar and at the bottom were strange loops as if the victim of this cross would not be nailed but held down by bands of steel.

Catching herself Claire said, "Sorry for staring. I've never seen a cross quite like that, what's the significance of the loops?"

He seemed pleased by the question and said, "It's the way we will get to heaven. You could too if you wanted. Are you Christian?"

She shook her head and said, "No I like sleeping in on Sundays."

The answer confused him and for a moment he simply stood open mouthed. Claire had always felt religion to be a private business. If this boy wore his religion like some kind of label that was his business. She was not about to join in the game.

"Oh, well thank you again," he stammered.

He left the room looking slightly deflated.

Good line Miss Anderson," said another student who'd been standing close enough to hear.

"I have a few. Mind you for the record I didn't mean to be flippant I just consider religion discussion on anything other than an academic level to be socially inappropriate," she explained. "Its way to easy for people to be hurt."

She was now the center of attention for a cluster of ten young people. Their wardrobes varied from casually conservative to vaguely exotic. Several of them she recognized as having asked very interesting and intelligent questions. The one who had spoken was a young twenty something woman with relatively conservative but stylish clothes and a small sparkling stud in one nostril.

"What's the story with him anyway?" she asked. "He seems like a bright kid but a bit fixated."

"He's ok. He was already a Christian when he started school but when he went home last summer he got in with this strange group."

Claire frowned at the news.

"This is not good," she said.

"I know but he still mixes in with everyone he used to and he talks to his family so it can't be as bad as some. He just spends all his long weekends at this retreat."

Claire shrugged and shouldered her purse. The teacher, like his counterpart at the first school, had been rather puzzled by her lack of written notes. That puzzlement had turned to understanding as she had started talking. If you lived your notes every day you really didn't need to write them down.

"Oh well, there's worse things he could be doing I guess."

A boy in jeans and a simple blue t-shirt spoke up.

"We usually go for coffee after this class Ms. A. want to come along?"

Claire thought for a minute and said, "Ok sure, lead the way."

*****

Claire spent late Monday afternoon and early evening with the energetic young people, learning about their lives and talking writing. Returning to the hotel at a little after nine o-clock she picked up the phone sitting on a table by her hotel room window, and called Alan Rose.

"I know what the Philadelphia Experiment is supposed to have been. That is if it ever actually happened," she said.

Claire settled into a chair by the window and looked out at the small town's dark main street. The stores were closed and only a tavern two blocks up the street showed any sign of life. This was the difference in lifestyles, cities didn't sleep. Towns for the most part not only slept they tended to go to bed rather early.

"So do I," said Alan. "I rented the movie this afternoon. It's an all right kind of a C level science fiction. It has this ship just disappearing and then reappearing in the middle of the desert."

"That's a bit different than what the web had to say but you have the idea I think. You'll have to admit that gives it a definite connection," said Claire.

"Did you e-mail the FBI?" Alan asked.

"I did, after I found out what the alleged Philadelphia Experiment was. I say alleged because according to more than one web site I read through the navy firmly denies it ever happened."

Alan made a harrumphing sound at this statement and said, "When you talk about governments and armies lots of things that happen don't. But the more I think about this the more I believe this isn't being done by a government agency."

Claire turned from her view of the quiet street to face the quiet anonymity of the hotel room.

"Why do you say that?" she asked. "I mean I asked him that and he shook his head but why do you say it?"

"Claire, no government agency is going to conduct this kind of experiment so openly. Neither would they do it with someone who is so clearly unwilling. They'd be doing it in some kind of shielded facility where the beam or whatever you want to call it, is not going to send their man all over the map. The man being transported would be one of theirs, a volunteer."

Claire gave a small, embarrassed laugh. She picked up the television's remote control and played with it, grasping its solid reality as an antidote to this unreal conversation.

"What's so funny?" Alan asked.

She said, "Just listen to us. We're talking the impossible. I mean I saw it, this time I even saw him appear. But you, I don't know why you don't give me a referral to a head doctor."

Claire heard a deep sigh on the other side of the line. When Alan spoke again he sounded much like he did when he had talked of his problems with his parents.

"Claire believing the impossible isn't that hard. People do it all the time. Take you for instance. First of all you're a fantasy writer. You have to believe the impossible at least a little or your work would be unconvincing."

Claire pondered this and knew it made a kind of sense.

"Okay, so that's why I'm able to believe this but what about you?" she asked.

"If you start with a firm belief in god's wonders, then man's wonders really only take a certain amount of circumstantial evidence."

Claire giggled softly and said, "Alan you're a nut."

"Yeah but I'm good at it," he said echoing her good humor.

Claire said, "I'll call you when I get home."

"What? Not continuing the investigation?" Alan asked.

There was both disappointment and a faint challenge in his voice. Claire wished she could rise to meet that challenge but had no idea how.

"I think I've done everything I can," she said. "I'm just a writer Alan not some kind of adventure movie hero. You have any ideas?"

Disappointment showing in his voice Alan said, "Not a one I'm afraid. I wish I did. Good night."

Claire bid her friend good night and hung up the phone. Turning she looked out at the vaguely unsettling view of the near empty street. It made her think of all the things she could fill this dark avenue with and for a moment the prospect of sitting here and writing crossed her mind. Instead of writing she took the television converter and stretched out on the bed.

She propped herself up on a pile of hotel pillows and turned on the television. In an afterthought she went back to the window and closed the curtains.

She did not want to see anything that might come out of thin air this night. She just wanted to watch TV, rest and in the morning move on to the final school.

CHAPTER 10

Kevin St. John read the text of the e-mail for the third time. He looked from the e-mail to the photocopy of a tabloid article sitting in the center of his desk. He then up at the man who had handed him the papers and now sat in a chair next to his desk. The man was Jerry Grenville. They were partners who worked together in this North Carolina office of the FBI.

"This is him. This is my brother," Kevin said firmly.

"It does sound like it," Jerry said, clearly not quite as convinced. "They didn't know what to make of the thing in Washington but enough of the facts checked out for them to send it to us. The screen name leads to a web based mailbox. The computer records say it was created the same day the e-mail was sent and just used once."

Jerry paused for a moment watching as Kevin skimmed the text of the message yet again. Before handing the material over to his partner he had studied it almost as intently. He had some opinions but opinions and reality were sometimes two different things. He preferred to wait for evidence before drawing any firm conclusions.

"It's well written that's for sure," Jerry said. "A crazy anonymous source that can write. I wonder what the odds are for that?"

"Come on Jerry this is serious," Kevin said. "David vanished over a month ago. This is the first lead we've had."

Jerry leaned back in his chair searching his mind for words that were a comfortable mix of caring and professionalism.

He said, "This is not a lead Kevin. The only reason we have it at all is because the confirmation with the tabloid reporter checked out. They don't expect us to do anything. How can we?"

Kevin made an impatient huffing sound. It caused Jerry to frown slightly. Their working styles were complimentary and had so far proved very effective. His partner had a habit of making what could be described as quantum leaps in logic then working toward that goal. It was his job to reign him in and keep him on track. Usually it was easier. Not this time.

"OK so maybe you're right," Kevin allowed reluctantly. "But there has to be something happening here and I think my brother is caught up in it. How many men do you know have a tattoo like this on their butt?"

He held up his right hand and showed a ring. It was made of silver and had a circle like a crest. The circle was made up of an intricate pattern of twisting lines.

Jerry shook his head then shrugged and said, "That sort of pattern is pretty common these days."

"You're right it is but they have it around the arm for show not hidden away," Kevin said firmly.

Jerry processed this bit of abstract fact and found himself bending. His partner had a point. That didn't make him right but he had a point.

"Maybe you have something there but I honestly don't think he's vanished. I think he got himself a chance to infiltrate one of the nuttier militia groups out there and hasn't had a chance to get in touch with us. He did have permission to do that you know if he felt it necessary and got the chance."

"He may have had permission but he never would have done it without at least phoning me. He was just going to monitor and report any changes in the make-up and location of the various groups."

Jerry said; "Sometimes you get a chance to do something more."

Kevin St. John leaned back in his chair and looked from the papers on his desk to his partner. The man who sat beside his desk was being very logical and reasonable. He could very well be right. At the same time Kevin was sure of his facts.

"I know that. I also know David. He's been wanting to do some undercover stuff for a while. We both knew it might be hard to report in the usual ways so I set up some different methods totally unconnected with the FBI, ways for him to let me know he was all right. A couple are just old friends who agreed to let me know if they got a strange letter from someone they didn't know. Others are messages on different internet bulletin boards."

"He's the brawn you're the brain?" Jerry asked.

Kevin smiled sadly.

"Not exactly," he said. "But he's a hell of a big brother to try and keep up with, always was."

Jerry nodded understandingly and said, "It's like that sometimes in families. That doesn't make him a better agent Kevin. Sibling rivalry notwithstanding."

Kevin sighed deeply. His partner had just outlined a very old problem.

"Jerry, most of the time I'm just a hacker chaser. Considering the way the world is wired that's every bit as important as any other assignment. But it's not very glamorous. David has always managed glamorous without half trying."

"You make me glad my brothers a locksmith. The best he can one up me with is stories about lost keys to chastity belts."

Both partners laughed at this image and their mood lightened. When Kevin could speak again he wondered aloud.

"Let's attack this logically. If this is David why would he be wandering around the continent naked? If you're right and he's joined some kind of group could this be part of their entrance exam? Is it some kind of endurance test he has to pass?"

They began to talk over the possible truth behind the fantastic sounding report. With every possibility they pulled out a file detailing what the FBI knew of that group. Soon the desk was full of files detailing a small selection of the hundreds of group both religions and military that the FBI thought potentially dangerous to the public.

Kevin sipped a coffee and looked at the pile. It was a mountain of paper detailing the fanaticism of people uncomfortable with the maybes in life. Each group insisted that its way was the only rout to salvation either politically in this world or spiritually in the next.

His partner's assessment of the family dynamic he had grown up in was completely true. His big brother had been an all American football player. He held black belts in two different martial arts disciplines. At the same time he was also an intelligent man with a Masters in criminal psychology.

Even with a PHD in computer sciences and a black belt in Karate Kevin always felt like a pesky little brother following in his big brothers footsteps.

82

The fact that he spent most of his time on white collar computer crime made it even harder to get any kind of family recognition. Chasing down gun toting religious fanatics, drug smugglers or greedy kidnapers was so much easier to understand.

Jerry spoke pulling Kevin out of his self-indulgent daydream. The tone in his partner's voice had hinted at the beginnings of an idea.

"You know something just occurred to me," he said.

"What?" asked Kevin.

"I was thinking about that tabloid story. I wonder if there have been any other strange reports of naked men wandering around?"

Kevin considered this curious thought for a moment. It made sense yet he immediately saw a problem inherent in following the question up.

"If he's wandered around like that anywhere else wouldn't most of them be like this incident in Toronto?" Kevin said.

"Probably," said Jerry. "But I'm betting most people would call the cops when they saw a man wandering around in the nude. That's what the tabloid writer did though I'd bet you he phoned his editor first."

Kevin thought this over and found himself nodding slowly.

He said, "Providing anyone saw him at all your right. I got some paper-work to clean up. See what you can find."

Jerry went to his own desk and began working at the powerful PC that sat waiting for him. Kevin set the e-mail aside and concentrated for a time on the case he was working at before the arrival of this distracting interruption.

"Crap, is this ever strange!" muttered Jerry.

Kevin looked up from his work and asked, "What?"

Jerry held up a hand and gestured for his partner to join him.

"Come here, look at this. I scored big time, got a bunch of reports of naked men wandering around. Most of the reports are from tabloids but a few are from police blotters or legitimate papers. It started looking like a pattern so I plotted them on a map."

Kevin went to his partners' desk and looked at the computer monitor. His mouth fell open in surprise. A jagged line of small red dots ran from

83

Toronto down the east coast staying roughly in a line with the Canadian city. The dots were evenly spaced. Numbers marking dates for all but three made the first in Toronto the final at the location mentioned in the e-mail.

"What are the dots with the question marks?" Kevin asked.

He tapped the monitor at a point half way up the coast.

"There were no reports for that general location but the pattern was so clear I put them there as a guess that he was there but not seen," Jerry answered.

"Or not reported," guessed Kevin.

"Exactly," Jerry muttered. "It seems like every three to six days he shows up at a different spot."

"But is he doing it willingly and why?" asked Kevin.

Jerry shrugged and scratched his cheek thoughtfully and said, "I dunno Kev this is starting to look really strange. I'm not an expert but I know the basics. There's not a single group I've ever read about that would make anyone do something like this."

"Do I get to say I told you so yet?" Kevin asked.

He smiled at the look his partner had in his eyes. It was a look that marked the beginning of a chase. Jerry chewed his lower lip thoughtfully for a moment, eyes on his computer's monitor and the strange pattern.

"Maybe."

Jerry typed a command and a nearby printer spit out two pages. He stood and went to the printer. When he came back to the desk he handed one paper to Kevin.

He said, "You take half the list. Lets play some phone tag and see if the sources stories match with our e-mail messenger. If they match then I might be ready to upgrade that maybe to a yes."

*****

It was night. Rain fell on the small shed's roof. Inside the shed was a dark inky space perfumed by the chemical toilet one corner of the small room. The cot had a bare mattress and a single blanket. In the horrific weeks since he had been taken this had been the only covering they had provided.

David St. John ran the last of his piece of bread around the bowl in his hands getting the last bit of the stew it had contained. He put the crust in his mouth and chewed listlessly. They fed him respectably but dredging up any appetite at all was starting to get very hard.

He thought of the woman. The odds against actually running into her that second time had been astronomical. Not only had he run into her but she seemed to understand what was going on. Yet all he could think of to do was scribble in the dirt.

Standing looking up at her for the moment he had curiously summoned up the strength to wonder what he would say to her if he were free. He remembered the feeling and held onto it for a moment. It reminded him that this nightmare that would probably end in death. At the same time it said that out there in the real world there were still people who were ready to hold out a hand and help.

As true at that might be he hadn't tried to actually contact anyone but this woman. Horrific memories of the first time the experiment had been conducted had kept him as far as possible from any living thing. The consequences were just too horrific.

It had been a dog, just a stray dog. He had fallen to the ground in the middle of a parking lot behind a nameless building and the poor friendly little animal had come up to lick his face and wag his tail. Trembling from fear and the physical effects of the experiment he had held the small animal grateful for its comforting presence.

Then the beam had struck again pulling him back. The dog had come too, or most of it had come. The power level in the beam had been set for only one man. The result had been unspeakable.

The sounds of singing began outside his small wooden prison. They did this every evening. Just singing and standing in a circle around the windowless shed. At first he had yelled and cursed his defiance. Tonight he simply finished his supper and put the bowl and spoon through the small flap covered hole in the door.

Curling up on the cot in his blanket he leaned against the wall. Outside he heard a mutter of voices then the voices began to sing some hymn. His eyes began to burn with tears and soon they were slowly trailing down his face. He slid slowly down to the mattress and stayed curled in a ball.

The singing was better than the experiment. The experiment was better than the punishment sessions that had begun since his attempted escape.

It had gotten into the master's head that the "Blessed one" needed to be cleansed of sin so the experiment would work the way they wanted. In the interests of managing this they had begun every third night to force him into some act of contrition. Huddled shivering in the dark David St. John was beginning to think that death might be preferable over all.

CHAPTER 11

Claire arrived at the final college town on Wednesday morning. Taking the exit off the highway she drove through streets that reminded her faintly of old movie musicals; films where fresh faced small town young teens turned barns into theaters and put on a show. They were plots that were as far from reality then as they would be today but the idea that even something from that world had been real was a fascinating thought.

After driving the streets totally lost for almost forty minutes Claire finally located the town's main street. She checked into a small hotel in the center of town. The hotel itself was in an elegant old structure proud of its hundred-year history.

After an excellent lunch in the hotel's restaurant Claire asked for directions then got in her car and drove the short distance to the college. Parking in a visitor's lot she set off for a long walk through the park like grounds. Since she was here early it made sense to orient herself with the college layout.

Like the other two schools this institution was somewhat sparsely occupied during this its summer session. There were students however and Claire found herself indulging in a session of people watching. She progressed through the grounds enjoying the mix of old, very old and modern architecture. These buildings no doubt constructed in various waves of rebuilding and expansion seemed to be clustered around a scattering of open greens intended as meeting places.

As she strolled through the grounds an intrusive sound began to become distracting. It was the sound of a not too distant amplifying system. Frowning at this intrusion on the peace Claire found herself wanting to locate the source of the sound, if only to tell them to turn it down.

Surrendering to her curiosity Claire followed the indistinct echoing voice to a plaza of brick surrounded by a green space. Here she found a man in his early twenties standing on a small wooden platform with a microphone in his hands. The now intelligible words could clearly be heard as part of a prose-lytizing fundamentalist Christian sermon.

Listening to this young man preach were three distinctive types of people standing in rough rings. The inner circle were clearly made up of near entranced devotees. Many of these faithful were wearing the odd looking out sized metal cross she had seen worn by the young writer at the last school.

It was a fact that made her anger at their interrupting her quiet walk with their noise vanish. Here was a chance to find out a bit about what motivate the oddly intense young student of the previous school.

The next circle standing outside these believers were clearly religious thinkers themselves but not members of the same sect. They seemed to be taking the speaker very seriously. Several asked questions Claire utterly failed to see the point about. The preacher's answers were just as abstract. These people knew what they were talking about. The jargon and short form references they used left Claire totally lost.

The final and largest of the groups were the disinterested unbelievers. This group simply stood on the paved plaza or sat on one of the benches surrounding this speaker's corner or they were stretched out on the grassy lawn. Most were amused by the young preacher's performance, a few were annoyed and some were openly hostile. Declaring surrender in the battle to understand what on earth the faithful were debating Claire began to study this last group.

A man stood watching. He was dressed casually with a school sweatshirt over new looking jeans. He had short black hair and a close cut beard shot slightly with white. He was the right age to be a teacher yet his bearing held a different quality. His dark eyes scanned the crowd in a way that made Claire think of a bird of prey waiting for some rodent to make one last wrong step.

Claire went to stand next to this interesting man. As she did so she was immediately aware that she had in turn become a topic of his interest. She listened to the speaker for a moment letting the man beside her study her at his leisure then she spoke.

"Are you with this group or just filling time?" she asked.

When the man spoke his accent brought the sound of the urban north to this southern spot.

"Jim Young chief of campus police," he said.

She glanced over at him to watch him take an identification wallet out of a pants pocket and showed it to her. He took his time slipping it back into his pocket clearly waiting for her to introduce herself. She obliged aware that it was probably part of his job to assess outsiders wandering through the campus.

"I'm Claire Anderson," she said. "I'm a writer due to speak here on Monday."

The all business look on the man's face melted. He smiled widely and extended his hand in greeting. Claire found his grip to be warm, firm and friendly.

"Oh yes! Claire Anderson, down all the way from Toronto, pleased to meet you. I didn't think you were expected till Sunday," he said expansively.

She said, "I'm not but I was given three schools to speak at and they all had the same schedule. Party Sunday night, classes Monday each one a week apart. It's given me some time to simply wander around and take a look at a part of continent I might simply have driven past otherwise."

"Well we're pleased to have you Ms. Anderson," he said. "This is a nice little town but it does tend to be simply on the way somewhere. Hope you enjoy your stay. I went and bought your book the other day when they announced you'd be coming. It's a good read."

"Thanks, please call me Claire. Does a small school like this really need its own police force?"

He shrugged and cased his eyes around their well- manicured surroundings and said, "We aren't UCLA or anything like that but whenever you get a respectable amount of teens and twenty-something's out on their own with only marginal adult influence you tend to attract your share of problems. I have almost as many men under me as the town sheriff."

He nodded to a man leaning against a tree a small distance away from the crowd. The man, dressed in a blue blazer with what looked like the school crest on the chest also appeared to be watching the crowd. He nodded back and continued to watch from where he stood. Jim Young stepped away from the crowd.

"He's one of mine. I don't normally hover over events like this but I was on my way past and got distracted. Show you around the campus?" Jim explained.

"If it's not too much trouble Mr. Young," Claire said.

"Call me Jim."

He led the way down a paved path that trailed away from the crowd. Claire walked at his side.

He said, "I need to get back to my office and I might as well take the long way around as any other. It's too nice a day to be stuck inside doing paperwork all day."

It was soon clear to Claire that this path would take them through what appeared to be the central part of the campus. That meant they would probably get where they were going fairly soon and she wanted to satisfy her curiosity with regard to this interesting man.

"You're not from around here." Claire observed.

"Now there's a sharp observation," he said. "I'm from New York, Brooklyn to be exact. I took my masters in history so naturally I became a cop."

"Makes sense," Claire observed. "For someone from Brooklyn that is."

"Ha, ha, very funny. I took two majors for my undergrad degree criminology and history. I wasn't quite ready to settle down so I went on and did the masters while I was trying to figure out if I wanted to become a cop or a lawyer. Anyway I was a detective by the time my kids began to get old enough to walk to school on their own. I started getting paranoid. It's safer down here. Not as safe as people might think but a big step up from Brooklyn."

"I don't blame you," Claire said. "Cities can be a mine field. I have friends with kids I have no idea how they do it without having nervous breakdowns. What about down here what do you spend most of your time dealing with? What's the big problem in this idyllic small town spot."

He thought for a moment then held up three fingers, lowering them as he listed his issues.

"Booze mostly for one," he began. "Next there's drugs, beyond that there's testosterone crazed football players that don't understand that no really does mean no."

"The big three. How about race problems?" Claire asked.

"They exist but times are changing," Jim said. "Around here the problems have always been just as much money oriented as race. The school runs a peer awareness and reconciliation program that usually keeps things from getting to the point where I might have to do something."

Claire glanced behind them. They had wandered out of sight of the preacher and his congregation but a faint echo of his sermon still drifted with the breeze.

"Why are you watching that group?" she asked. "You and your man that is."

Jim Young rolled his eyes in a clear picture of exasperation. He pinched the bridge of his nose as if to stem the tide of an emotion charged outburst. Sighing deeply he shoved his hands in his pockets.

"Religious cults on campuses have been a problem all over the states since the sixties. Canada too though up there things aren't quite as extreme. Around here we get some real winners. This area is what they call the Bible belt. Fundamentalism is the norm here. To get any attention at all your average cult has to do some far out public relations."

They stopped walking in front of what was one of the older college buildings. A brass plaque next to the door marked it as housing administration offices. Claire's companion sat down on a bench that was next to the main entrances Claire sat next to him. He crossed his arms and looked around as if seeing the problems he knew were there just underneath the peaceful surface.

"Sounds like a difficult problem," Claire observed. "How do you handle that sort of thing?"

"We do what you saw today," Jim said. "Keep an eye on whatever group is operating and shoo away the nuttier ones. When they're spotted that is, some of them do a damn good job of hiding. We also make sure the ones that seem to have their feet somewhere near the ground have permits before they set up their podiums on campus grounds. Constitutional freedoms of religion and assembly being what they are that's the best that can be done."

Claire cocked a thumb in the general direction of the way they had come.

"What about this one? I saw the cross they wear up close at the last school I spoke. It's rather odd. So's their story line. I didn't understand half of what that kid said but some of the bible reading kids seemed pretty put out," she observed.

"The group is called, The Power and The Blood. Sometimes they call themselves, The Doorway to Heaven. I have a guy on staff who's a bible reading Baptist, knows his chapters and verses backwards. He calls them boarder line heretical. They're defiantly regional, that boy you saw must come from around here. They own a lot of land in the hills west of here where they have some kind of retreat."

An edge in her companion's voice seemed to echo Claire's concern.

"It seems like they bother you," she observed.

He said, "They're highly organized, and well-funded, almost military in the way the run things. They have defiant stages where they let their follow-ers learn just a little more about their secrets. Only the ones that are totally committed and have proven their loyalty get to go to the retreat."

"You find that sort of thing uncomfortable?" Claire asked.

Jim nodded slightly and said, "I'm not the only one either. An FBI agent was by here something like six weeks ago. They monitor groups like this all the time to make sure they don't turn violent. We had a couple meetings and he sat in on one of their preach and teach sessions."

Claire nodded toward the distant common.

"That's what that was?" she asked.

"Yup. He warned me to keep a close eye on them. He also recommend-ed the college should step up whatever any cult management programs it has. Which we have done."

"Sounds ominous," Claire observed.

"We're dealing with people's lives here," Jim said.

He made a sweeping gesture with one arm to take in what they could see of the campus.

"It may be hard to believe but even today a lot of college age kids can still be wide-eyed and innocent. They believe what they're told. If they're the slightest bit needy emotionally for whatever reason, homesick or boyfriend dumped them or new in town and having problems finding friends, they can fall for a cult's line before they even realized they're hooked."

Claire thought for a moment. She tended to treat her own faith like a comfortable old sweater she could put on and take off whenever she wanted. Though she could see herself becoming more observant as she got older the prospect of becoming as obsessed as this man was describing was something she could not understand.

"Is this group collecting guns like some of the ones you hear about out in Wyoming?" she asked.

Jim shrugged. For a moment he looked bothered not by the cult but by something else.

"I dunno, the Fed was supposed to look into that and give me a call. I guess he got distracted. It's possible he found there was nothing to be concerned about and just moved on."

Claire frowned at this. It seemed a departure in protocol from a man who at first sounded very concerned for the young people in this school. In a book she would have called it a plot hole, action left unexplained by the author.

"He'd go on without telling you what he found?" she asked.

"Sure. I'm just a campus cop he doesn't need to check in with me. He only got in touch with me to begin with because that group started bothering him and he wanted to warn me about them."

Claire got to her feet and Jim followed her example. It wasn't her business to tell this professional how to do his job and she was just a bit afraid that if she didn't move on she might try. The plot hole had an explanation; it might even be the right one. Of course the alternate explanation she had to offer was completely impossible.

"I see, well it's been nice meeting you," she said.

"I'll see you Sunday afternoon then," he said.

"You'll be at the reception?" she asked.

"Wouldn't miss it for the world. I'll bring my book for you to sign."

He gave her a warm friendly smile then entered the building. Claire looked back the way she had just come. For a moment the campus had the look of a stage setting waiting for her fertile mind to deliver it a plot. The problem was the plot that came to mind was purely fantastic reality.

He had come here. He had gotten too close to some secret. They had taken him and were now using that secret but why?

She shook her head and began to walk back to her car. She was a writer of adventures not an adventurer. Even if she did make the mental leap that said the disappearing man was this same missing FBI agent. Even if she tried the odds against this pragmatic man being as open minded, as Alan was astronomical. Faced with the likelihood of his total disbelief there was simply nothing she could do.

CHAPTER 12

By the time Claire found her way back to her car the young preacher and a selection of followers were loading the disassembled podium and sound system into a small van parked in the same lot. They worked with quiet efficiency and the ease of long practice. A quick glimpse of metal caught her eye and she realized that a few of these adherents were wearing something more than the cross.

"Have you been saved?"

Claire jumped slightly. The speaker was a young woman who had noticed her watching the job of loading the van. She had asked a question Claire had no idea how to answer. Seeing her confusion the girl changed her tactics.

"Are you a Christian?" she asked.

She was an ordinary looking girl of about nineteen or twenty. Stick thin she would have made a model quiet easily but for her rather drab body covering clothes and a slightly glassy pinched look to her eyes. Claire's answer to her question slipped out without any thought.

"No I'm a reform Druid," she said. "We think praying to trees is a bit ostentatious. We pray at bushes."

The girl's eyes widened slightly. She took a half step back clearly startled. Claire had to struggle to not laugh. The whole performance reminded her of a character in a monster movie, the sort that screams the loudest and then gets eaten by the monster first.

"You're a pagan?" the girl asked.

"No dear I'm Jewish. That was a joke."

Claire was immediately sorry she'd been quite so self-indulgent. The girl clearly taking the remark far too seriously was frowning slightly as if she wondered whether there was a difference between pagan and Jew. She appeared to shake the thought off and smiled.

"Is there something I can tell you about our faith?" she asked.

"I am a little curious. Some of your company here seem to be wearing what look like iron bracelets. You don't though," Claire observed.

"Those are the seniors," she whispered conspiratorially. "They know about the truth. We're going to heaven soon."

Claire frowned at this statement and for a moment visions of poison laced fruit punch danced in her head.

"You're a bit young to be talking like that aren't you?" she asked.

The girl giggled and when she spoke again she sounded like a teenage baby sitter explaining why a child had to go to bed.

"You don't have to die to go to heaven silly! You just have to be able to open the door."

A strong male voice made the girl jump slightly. It was the young preacher. In the square he had been using a sound system but it was clear he had well developed vocal skills and would seldom have any problems making himself heard.

"Bid the woman God bless and come along Sally-May. Time to go," he said.

Sally-May ran to the van without looking back. The young preacher helped her into the van. After a stiff and slightly wary nod farewell he got into the front passenger seat and they drove away.

*****

That evening sitting and looking out the window of her hotel room Claire found herself pondering the painfully thin young girl and her companions. Picking up the phone she called Alan Rose. He was alone this time and sounded faintly as if he were either engrossed in a book, or a television program.

"Alan have you ever gotten into the business of cult deprogramming?" she asked.

"Now that's out of left field," he said. "It's hardly a business but I've been involved in it a little, more from the point of preventative lectures than deprogramming. I have a friend who does the real thing full time. He works

96

for a foundation set up by some people who lost their kids to cults back in the sixties. Why the interest?"

Claire detailed the conversation she had with Jim Young. She then began to described the encounter with the wide eyed Sally-May.

"You told her you were a WHAT?" he exclaimed.

Alan started laughing. By the time Claire finished her story he was still emitting stifled giggles.

"Alan, you're laughing at me long distance," she prodded gently.

"I'm sorry," he gasped. "You're something else you really are. I wish I'd been there. Did you think that one up on the spur of the moment?"

Claire smiled at a selection of very old memories.

"No I can't claim that one. My mother used to say it whenever the Seventh day Adventists knocked at the door. When the kid fed me the line the whole thing just came out," she admitted.

"I may use it."

Clare pulled a chair to the window and sat looking out. This town's main street had an appealing modern bustle. It made the subject of this conversation feel that much stranger.

"Feel free. Do you think this friend of yours would know about this group? The campus cop described them as being very local," she asked.

"I'll give him a call and ask him. It's hard to tell though. That boy you described, in the other school. You say he keeps in contact with his family?"

"That's what the other kids said," said Claire. "I spent most of the early evening with them and that's all they could tell me about it. Mind you, I wasn't that interested at the time."

"If that's the rule with most of them my friend might not know much more than your police chief. Parents don't usually resort to deprogrammers unless their kids have turned their backs on the world completely."

Claire sighed and rubbed her left temple. She was beginning to get the same feeling she got when the bits and pieces of a plot were coming together. Only she this time she wasn't writing a book.

"Give him my cell number anyway will you?" she said. "He might know something. This is too close to be a coincidence."

"I know. I was thinking about that as you were talking," Alan said. "You're not going to do anything stupid are you?"

It was Claire's turn to laugh.

"Don't worry Alan. I write about heroes, fictional heroes. I don't have the right stuff to actually be one."

*****

The shed door opened. David St. John sat on his bed elbows on knee's head in his hands. He didn't look up. It was time again for that short stretch of painful freedom. Time for the experiment.

"Blessed one come out," his escort intoned giving the command the weight of scripture.

"Torturing bastards, come in and get me!" he yelled.

They came, two large men. He had fought them at first but now he simply hung in their arms making it difficult to move him from the small black room into the comparative brightness of the compound.

He looked around as they pulled him along a path lined on both sides with people. Most were men but in the back rows he could see women. They were all in a passion of religious ecstasy.

Each member of this congregation held a long thick candle. The tunnel of flickering light this created led from the shed/prison to a large hanger like building. As they approached the large door to the building opened and the company could see the equipment it contained.

Four men in lab coats pushed a large dish antenna mounted on a wheeled platform out onto the hard-packed dirt of the space in front of the building. They adjusted the skyward angle in which the dish pointed and stepped aside. This made it easier for the company to see the device within.

The Master stood in front of this device. He wore a long white robe. Around his wrists and ankles were steel bands. Around his neck hung a steel cross. Behind him was something that looked very much like a huge steel egg.

He moved to a control panel and pressed a button. The lid to the egg lifted up. Inside was a man sized cross.

David St. John looked at the cross and felt a surge of memory born fear. He began to fight the strong hands that held him. They were ready for this and others stepped out of the throng and lifted him up. Bodily they carried him to the great egg stepping over the edge of the bottom to get to the cross inside.

First they placed him on the cross. They removed the shackles on his ankles and used an iron band to hold his legs to the body of the cross. Then they removed the handcuffs stretched out his arms and clamped his wrists down firmly. The feel of the cold hard steel beneath his body gave David St. John the strength to try again to reason with the unreasonable force that had held him here for so long.

"When are you people going to believe me? The only way this thing is going to send anyone to heaven is by killing them!"

Deaf to his victim's words the old man held his hands out to the congregation. Expectantly they fell quiet.

"Once I was a young man and wore my country's colors. I was given the privilege of taking part in a great experiment. They were risking our lives but such is the fate of any soldier. But I had heard rumors. This was not just a risk this was certain death. I resolved to save myself. I put on a life preserver and stood at the edge of the deck if there was danger I could jump. I did jump. Before I jumped I was in a haze of wonder beyond that was a light. It was a light that was the face of God!"

"It wasn't God dam-it!" screamed St. John.

The old man and the congregation continued in their well-rehearsed ceremony ignoring their desperate victim's protestations. Technicians stood at control panels one at the dish and the other at the device itself.

"Why don't you listen to me? It wasn't God!" David yelled. "It was the magnetic field hitting your brain cells and registering in your mind as light! All you people are doing is sending me around the country! I'm not going through time. I'm not going into any other dimension. I'm not getting anywhere near God! Will you please for pity sake put a bullet in my head and get it over with!"

As if to counteract his victims disbarring statement the old man began to put some extra feeling into his words. His enraptured followers hung on his every word.

"Twenty four hours later I was pulled from the water by two good men. As I accepted their aid I knew what I had to do. I came home to these mountains and prayed to God and studied to understand. God sent me good fortune and I bought this land."

With a sweeping gesture the old man indicated the equipment he stood in front of.

"That God will not much longer stand behind the vale. For God has guided my hand in all that I have done. God has brought me to this time and place so I might show all the way to step beyond that vale. It was done once my friends and it will be done again!"

The technician at the device declared, "Full power!"

The one at the dish said, "Angle is set and ready."

The old man waved a hand to his followers who obediently knelt in prayer.

To the technicians he said, "Begin."

"This is a farce damn-it," David yelled. "When are you going to listen to me?"

David St. John helplessly watched the candle lit compound disappear behind the dome of steel. After a moment a force gripped him. It felt like an electric shock, strong enough to bring pain but at the same time did not burn. The pain grew and he found himself screaming out his agony and hearing his own voice echoing within the steel tomb. Then the pain was gone and he was somewhere else.

CHAPTER 13

"Have you heard the good word?"

Sally-May Le Blank tried hard to keep her mind on the mission at hand. She and her preaching team were standing at scattered positions outside the big mall located between the town and the interstate highway. They were here handing out pamphlets, or to be more precise they were trying to hand out pamphlets. There weren't many takers.

Sally looked around. It was a warm sunny day she was on her own and for once she was glad. The men in the group were strong moral and very dependable. There weren't always drinking and trying to push you into sex. But sometimes, just sometimes, they made her feel like a child, always in need of meeting their approval.

A dark memory interrupted the beautiful morning.

"My name is David."

His voice, muffled by the door, had sounded weak in physical strength but strong in spirit. Was that a bad thing or a good thing? Was strength the same thing as pride?

A woman and two children walked past. Sally-May held out one of her leaflets. She smiled as she did so it always helped.

"Have you read the good news?"

The woman passed without comment. The brief encounter barely slowed Sally-May's inner dialogue. She kept thinking, pondering the nature of strength.

Her father had thought strength was the same as pride. Her father had thought his wife and two daughters had been full of pride and that was the sin he seemed to despise the most. His lessons in humility had been many and varied.

Now a different voice replaced the imprisoned man's.

"I'm getting out of here Sally-May. I won't tell you where so you won't have to lie to daddy. I promise when I find a job and get a place I'll send for you."

Everyone knew that her older sister Alison had run away some shortly after she turned sixteenth. She had been two years younger, full of envy at her sister's strength. She'd been there when she walked out the door but a soft voice in the back of Sally's mind said something else happened. The voice muttered to her softly regarding the events of that evening over five years ago. There was no proof yet something insisted that things had not ended with Alison LeBlanc simply walking out the door and down the path to the road. The simple fact was their father never lost a fight, ever.

The soft voice always spoke of the outhouse. It was the place where the hired help that worked on their big dairy farm answered nature. The day after Alison left, her father moved the small shed and filled in the hole himself. It had been years since he had done anything even close to this kind of menial labor. A short while later he planted a tree on top of the spot. A cherry tree, her sister's favorite.

"These things just aren't sanitary," he had said to his remaining child's hesitant questions. "It's about time this place had a proper toilet for the help. We can put it in the storage shed. It's a good location for it and it'll be lots warmer in the winter too."

Sally-May pushed the dark dream from her mind but a different one appeared as a replacement. Her mother fell ill soon after she moved away and started college. It was almost as if the strength necessary for getting her only remaining child safely out of the house had drained her past recovery. Their final conversation had been a difficult one over the phone with more unsaid than said.

"You need to promise me girl. You need to promise me never to come back. Not even if I die. You just stay where you are and pray for my soul like I pray for yours."

Her father's voice interrupted these faintly gasped instructions. He grabbed the phone away out of his sickly wife's hand. Like an old time preacher he did not so much as talk as pronounce.

"Sally-May why am I paying for a nurse to tend your mother when she has a daughter who should come home and do right by her? You get back here girl. You get back here right now!"

A man and a little boy got out of a car. They walked near where Sally-May was standing. Shaking her father's voice from her mind Sally held out one of her tracts. That was the past, this was now.

"Have you heard of the Power and the Glory?"

The boy, no older than four, took the paper but the father took it out of his hands and handed it back.

"No thank you."

Sally watched the two males one young, one adult walk into the mall. She wondered about men. Did they all expected you to take after them like shadows? Were there any who only wanted you to be with them as equals? The thought made her feel very tired.

She was at school on a full scholarship and studied hard so that her grades stayed high enough to keep that funding. At the same time she worked long hours for the master and his seniors. Sometimes the combination made her so tired she wondered if anything she said made sense.

At the same time she knew without a doubt that getting to heaven was very important. She would be with her mother, maybe with her sister if the tall and sweetly blooming cherry tree on her father's farm covered what she thought it covered. Her devil of a father would be far, far away.

Sally-May's drifting distracted eyes caught on a car coming into the parking lot and followed it to where it stopped. The car's driver was strangely familiar. The woman was half way to the place were Sally stood when she remembered where she had seen her first.

This woman was the person who had made that strange joke. Religion was not something to joke about. God was the ultimate father and there was no moving away from him. You had to take God's rules seriously or something worse than you could ever imagine could happen.

The woman reached where Sally-May was standing. Sally-May smiled and held out her hand. Here was a soul that really needed her attention.

"Have you heard the good news?"

The woman took the pamphlet. She looked at it for a long moment and appeared to actually be reading the message on the cover. Sally's heart thumped extra hard.

"What makes this news so good?" she asked.

Sally-May smiled widely at the woman and a surge of excitement made her grip the bundle of pamphlets in her hand so hard they bent in half. Finally, for the first time that day a chance to do some one on one preaching.

"I can tell you all about it if you'd like," she said.

The woman smiled kindly. Just for a moment, a fleeting second, the kindness made Sally-May want to cry.

"Why don't you come in and walk around the mall with me? While we're at it we could have some lunch," the woman said. "My treat."

Sally-May's reaction to the kindness in the woman's eyes was replaced in her mind by the pragmatic logistics of where they were. She didn't want to cry anymore, she simply sighed in frustration.

"We're not supposed to go into the mall," she explained. "We did at first but they called the police. We can't come nearer to the doors than this."

The woman waved the explanation away as if it were a feather and said, "Oh that's easy to fix. Just stuff those papers into your bag and walk with me. You won't be preaching you'll just be shopping. They can't stop that can they?"

Sally-May's mouth fell open. Catching herself she closed her mouth and thought this over for a moment then nodded uncertainly.

"I guess they can't," she said. "You're right."

Sally stuffed the bundle of pamphlets in her hands into the big purse she carried and smiled at the woman who led the way toward the nearest set of doors. She held the door open for Sally-May to enter.

"You're Sally-May am I right?" the woman asked.

Sally-May stopped, wondering at the woman's knowledge, the words of a sermon on dark angels with all the knowledge of the world running through her mind.

"How did you know?" she asked hesitantly.

"You're friend called you to the car yesterday remember?" she said. "He used your name."

Sally-May blushed and entered the mall.

"Oh, I guess he did. You remembered?"

The woman entered the mall leaving the door to slowly close behind them.

"I'm a writer," she explained. "Things like that stick in my mind sometimes."

*****

Claire smiled to herself. There was nothing missing in this girl that a lot of good strong mentoring and some decent food couldn't go a long way toward fixing. She was twenty years old but seemed much younger. Claire reflected that clinging to absolutes sometimes had that effect.

The more Sally-May talked about those absolutes the more Claire wondered about her. Deep down there was something very lonely and empty about this young woman. Every time she set off on a tangent, reciting the dogma of this cult of hers Claire wondered why she had picked this particular subject to do the filling. They passed a store and Claire remembered that she was here for more than just a cheap lunch.

"Hang on I need some nylons," she said. "I put my toe through my last pare. Not that I wear them very often I'm more of a sock person."

They entered a store and Claire made a show of standing at a rack of hose before picking a pair of black pantyhose. Skimming the particulars on the back of the package to make sure this was her size she said;

"I've always wondered about people who claim they have the truth. How do they know it's the truth? Maybe this master of yours just has a very vivid imagination."

Sally-May seemed to understand what she was getting at but still held fast to her doctrine.

"Oh no it's nothing like that," she said. "He really knows. He's seen things."

Claire chose two packages of hose and took the stockings to the cash counter. She probably wouldn't need more than one but she really didn't wear them very often. She had to allow for putting her thumb through the first pair while putting them on.

As she went she said, "I have a cousin who used to see things. The doctor gave him these little pink pills, fixed him right up."

The girl made an impatient noise at this.

"Medicine is wrong. God might have been gifting your cousin with blessed visions. Those pills could have been counter to Gods will and that's a terrible sin."

Claire sighed deeply and shook her head. She paid for the stockings and led the way out of the store.

"Sally the only message we ever got out of my cousin, while he was still very sick that is, consisted of his deeply felt conviction that the cat was an agent of the CIA. Rather creative thinking for a dentist but not, I think, very useful theology."

Claire sat on a mall bench and found a place in her purse for her hose. Sally-May slowly sat down beside her. The girl seemed to be struggling with some difficult concept. Claire waited for her to speak. Independent thought was a tricky business and when done without practice tended to take time.

"I'm not sure I understand. Are you a believer or aren't you?" she asked.

It was a fair question. Eyes on the mall crowds that rushed walked or simply ambled past their bench Claire thought over her answer. At the same time she wondered if there was a way to explain what she personally thought in a way that was both honest and might also reach this young woman. The rainbow pattern on a little girls dress gave her an idea.

"Sally do you know the story of Noah's ark?" she asked.

"Of course everyone knows that," Sally-May said.

She sounded annoyed as if she felt she was being mocked. Claire smiled at this. It showed a level of perception that just might help this girl find her way to mental freedom.

"Yes but do you know what the end product of that story is?" Claire prodded.

"We must obey gods will or his wrath is terrible," Sally said.

Here was the notion of god as vice principal, ready to paddle the unwary. Not a nice picture or from what she personally was taught a very complete one.

"Why did God put the rainbow in the sky?" Claire asked simply.

Sally-May opened her mouth but appeared to be at a loss. Claire smiled and knew she had picked the right message.

"Why did God put the rainbow in the sky?" she repeated.

Sally-May's mouth opened and closed once, twice. Claire guessed she wanted to repeat more of her force fed dogma but was bright enough to know it wasn't to the question. Now was the time to deliver her real message.

"Sally the end lesson of that story is very simple. God gave men free will. Thinking for yourself and having an independent mind is part of what God is all about. Oh sure you end up with doubts sometimes. A lot of the time really. That's the price of owning that thing God gave you, your own mind."

Claire paused for a moment to see how this idea was settling into this woman's consciousness. She was listening intently looking off at some invisible point somewhere in midair. Claire pressed her point hoping this was the right time and not too soon to try and get what she wanted. She had read that real cult deprograming took hours or days yet one clear understandable doubt could start the ball rolling.

She asked, "Sally do you own your own mind or have you leased it out? I've listened to you talk for about twenty minutes now and all I've heard are parroted words first created by someone else."

The girl's suddenly haunted eyes began to scan the people in the mall as if looking for some answer to the question she had been handed. Claire knew she was looking in the wrong place. The answer was inside.

"Sally as I said before I'm a fantasy writer. To get ideas for my work I often read about different myths and religions. It's a fascinating subject. I don't think I've read about one faith that does not hold to that basic tenant, do unto others only that which you would like done to you. Much of the rest is just window dressing created by culture and invented by men to support class differences and sex role stereotypes. I'm not saying don't believe in God. When you get right down to it I think I probably do believe. What I'm saying is you have to think very, very carefully when you start to believe in men."

The young woman sat hands limply in her lap. For a moment it almost looked like she had decided not to think anything at all. Then she was very clearly thinking of something and a single tear ran down one cheek.

She jumped to her feet stepping away from the bench. Claire saw the look in her eyes and knew for now she had probably lost this fight. Losing the war itself was another thing. The war would be fought inside this young woman's head and that was something Claire could do little about.

"I, I must go," Sally-May stammered. "They'll be looking for me. It's time to go back to town. I have classes this afternoon."

"Why not have lunch with me? My treat," Claire offered. "I'm in town to give a talk at the university next Monday and I'd love the company. I'll drive you straight to your class."

"Thank you ma'am but no."

She turned and almost ran down the corridor to the nearest doors. Claire shook her head at the sight. She knew it was unrealistic to hope for some kind of talk show instant recover but it was still disappointing to see this girl run away so completely from what she had to offer.

"So close and yet so far."

Claire watched the girl till she disappeared into the crowd. She stood and wandered in the direction of the nearest map. It took her a bare minute to regain her sense of direction and she began walking in search of food. It was way past time for lunch.

CHAPTER 14

Claire found the mall's food court and immediately felt right at home. It looked just like every other food court in any other mall in North America. Sometimes that kind of sameness saddened her. After losing track of the delicate and confused young Sally-May this sameness was curiously comforting.

Young people might throw their lives away. Religion might play the part of cage instead of comfort. Some things at least were dependable. There would always be malls, and in those malls there would be pizza, Chinese food and burgers. The seating would be just slightly uncomfortable. The green and healthy looking plants would be plastic and any ratty sickly looking greenery would be alive.

Contemplating the slightly poetic nature of these facts Claire picked Chinese food. In short order she was carrying a tray with stir-fried beef, bean sprouts and rice. A bottle of ice tea balanced precariously next to the plate. It smelled good and actually looked appetizing.

Claire carried this bounty to a far corner of the increasingly crowded common eating area. Here she sank onto a padded bench on one end of a long row of tables. It was getting close to twelve and the place was filling up.

Roughly half of her meal had been eaten when a ringing erupted from her purse. Frowning in confusion Claire fumbled for the instrument. Congratulating herself for finding the thing while it was still ringing she answered.

"Hello?"

"Is this Claire Anderson?" said a voice she didn't know.

"That's me. What can I do for you?" she asked. Belatedly she added, "Pardon my chewing in your ear. I'm in the middle of lunch."

She swallowed what was in her mouth and then concentrated on the voice on the phone. She'd gotten to the point in her carrier where phone calls could come from almost anywhere. That being the case it was politic to listen first and make judgments on the value of the call later.

The voice said, "No problem. I'm George Applebee, Alan Rose asked me to call you."

A light of memory went on in Claire's head.

"Oh, you're the deprogrammer. I'm so glad to hear from you," she said.

The soft laugh in her ear was warm and friendly.

He said, "That's what I've been called among other things though there's not much of that done these days. The groups I deal with know what lines not to cross so they stay under the radar of people like me. I'm told you're interested in finding out about a group called The Power and The Blood. I had some time so I thought I'd give you a call."

Claire said, "Glad you did, I just had a long talk with a young lady who was handing out pamphlets. She seemed very bright and totally committed but it also seemed like she hadn't thought to deeply about what she was committing herself to. It was a frustrating conversation. I thought I was starting to get to her but in the end she crawled back into her shell and ran off."

His answer to this description was guarded but positive. It was clear that he knew exactly the sort of thing she was talking. Listening she could tell he had probably lived the scene she had just experienced many times.

"It's possible you did touch her. It doesn't take much sometimes just the right word at the right time. Unfortunately unless you can take her completely away from the group, and I mean physically away, that sort of inner change can take a long time. Unless you're dealing with a minor moving someone can create legal problems. I've had associates up on kidnapping charges. None of them stuck because the cult didn't want the publicity but in one case it came to a near thing. As for your girl, it's a scary world and certainty is one of the things a cult hands its members. Of course then there's individual predisposition."

Claire found herself fascinated.

"What do you mean individual predisposition?" she asked.

George went on to explain this, his patient tone of voice reminding Claire of more than one of her favorite teachers. The man had never used a textbook, never worked from notes yet everyone who took his class stated that he had without exception been the best teacher they ever had.

"People who join cults are often running away from particular and very personal demons. I had one boy who left home and joined the Moonies. Don't know if you remember them, they got very big in the seventies. The father reportedly accepted the boy's choice of life. The mother came to me. My team and I got him alone after a little effort then went to work on him. It took three days and nights but we eventually found out that one of the reasons he left home in the first place was because his dad had been sexually abusing him."

"Which explains why the father didn't mind him running off," Claire grumbled taking a drink of her ice tea. "Better that than have him go to the cops."

George went on in a matter of fact tone that made Claire wonder exactly how many stories like this he had to tell. It was a question to which she realized she didn't want to know the answer.

"Anyway, on to your particular little group," George continued. "I don't know much about them. I've only talked to one member myself and that was in an advisory capacity rather than what you would call actual deprogramming."

"Advisory?" Claire asked, confused by the label.

"The subject was the son of a strict fundamentalist preacher. He's the leader of a group that itself is a border line cult," George explained. "The father respects my opinions even if he doesn't completely agree with my views. He asked if I would simply come to Sunday dinner and talk to his son. He didn't object to his son being involved in a different group but some of the things the boy was saying bothered him."

"Why?" Claire asked, remembering both her talk with Sally-May and the sermon of the day before.

"I didn't understand till I'd talked to the boy but some of the things this group says border on idolatry," George explained. "The Power and the Blood does not see going to heaven as a kind of abstract thing done by the soul.

They think of it as a physical event, like getting on a plane. It bothered the boy's father as being sinful. It bothered me for a whole different reason."

Claire thought of the pamphlet she still had in her purse. She hadn't read it, preferring to talk to the girl herself. She wondered did they actually tell this sort of fairy story to the potential convert on the street? That sort of thing seemed to be the carrot to hand out to devotees piece by piece in the interests of binding them to the faith. It also sounded like something considerably less innocent.

She said, "Sounds like that group that killed themselves so they could go off into space on a comet."

"Technically it was a space ship traveling behind the comment but that's exactly what I'm talking about. We need to keep an eye on this group or it's possible that a lot of people from around there are going to lose their sons and daughters," George said grimly.

Claire looked around at the swiftly filling food court and wondered how many of these ordinary looking people had relations who wore the strange metal cross.

"Is the boy still a member?" she asked.

"Our meeting happened the beginning of last summer. He'd just finished his freshman year. He wasn't happy with his major and that gave me a chance. With his parents help I talked him into going to a college up north where I have connections. My connections got him involved in a lot of different things running from amateur theater to stuffing envelopes for the young republicans."

Clare smiled thinking of an old joke. He would have heard it before but that was the best part of old jokes.

"You mean there really are young republicans?" she asked.

It was clear he had heard that one before.

"Ha, ha, very funny," he said. "Anyway these days he keeps his cross in the bottom of his sock drawer."

Claire smiled at the faint tone of satisfaction showing in George Applebee's voice. This was a man who knew how to savor victories, even small ones.

"A win for common sense and moderation," she said. "Congratulations. One down a couple thousand to go."

"This group isn't as big as some others thankfully," he said sounding philosophical. "In this case were talking about a few hundred rather than thousand, but you're right there's still a lot out there. I don't want them to give up on god Ms. Anderson. I'm a man of faith myself. I just want them to own their own minds."

"Don't worry Mr. Applebee I understand completely. Can I call you if I have any other questions?" Claire asked. "This is foreign soil to me in more ways than one and I may need a road map."

"By all means."

He gave her his number and Claire entered the number into her palm pi-lot. This done they said their good-byes and Claire put phone and palm pilot back into her purse.

The food court was now very full and noisy. Claire began to concentrate on what was left of her lunch, in the interests of getting away from the din. She was almost finished when a presence in front of her table caused her to look up.

It was a man in an ordinary suit and tie holding a tray with a burger and fries. His eyes were an arresting blue. His face caused a strange tickle of recognition to begin in the back of her mind.

"Ok if I sit here the place is kind of packed?" he asked.

"Sure go ahead," she said. "I'm almost finished anyway."

It was only when he sat that she noticed he was wearing an interesting piece of artwork on one finger. The artwork was in the form of a ring with a kind of insignia. The insignia was a circle of intertwining lines.

"That's a fascinating piece of artwork you're wearing," she said.

He looked at the ring and smiled. Looking at his face lent an extra heart thump to her chest. It was impossible but it seemed she'd seen this man before.

"My sister's a jeweler. She does all sorts of stuff mostly in silver. She did this for me when I graduated from Quanico."

"You're in the FBI," she asked.

The man nodded and took a bite of his burger. Claire thought of the missing man and all the things she had seen since the moment she had seen him standing at the beach end of her street. They were thoughts that made her tired and more than a little lost.

Feeling lost made her think of the other man she knew with arresting blue eyes. Thinking of him she remembered the long and elaborate e-mail. She wanted to know if there was a connection with her message and this man and there was only one way to tell.

Struggling to keep her voice light and casual she said, "You know I once saw a man with a tattoo just like that on his left buttock."

The moment the last word left her mouth she desperately wished it unsaid. He was sitting across from her mouth hanging open, as if she had just confessed to a murder.

CHAPTER 15

Sally-May sat in the front passenger seat of the mini-van. The wheels spun on the black top making a soothing hum. Her mind was spinning counter clockwise dancing with the unwelcome phantom of doubt. Pushing doubt from her mind she tried to concentrate on the sound of the wheels on pavement. Instead of a soothing hum the sound carried the memory of a voice on the other side of a locked door.

"My name is David."

John Hugh sat next to her his back stiff as if he still felt his discomfort with amount of time it had taken for them to find her. Finally he spoke his voice firm but without anger. They had apparently been waiting for her for a full ten minutes before she appeared at the mall entrance.

"You left your post Sally-May," he said calmly. "We were worried. Did you find a person to minister to?"

Sally-May was glad she could answer his question honestly. At the same time she knew that she had no intention of telling him the whole truth. It wasn't like her yet oddly it felt good to have some private adventure to keep for her own.

"Yes I did," Sally said. "It was a woman. The same one I was talking to after the meeting. She suggested that I put my flyers in my purse so we could walk in the mall and talk without bothering the mall security. I thought it was a good idea so that's where I was. I don't think we'll see her though. She was very stubborn and said a lot of troubling things about faith."

John shook his head at this answer. For a moment Sally-May had a rush of fear. He had seen through her occasional silences more than once, knowing that she was hiding some small thing that was troubling her. Did he know she was troubled by more than just what the woman had said?

"Most in this world are blind Sally-May. We must be charitable with them after all think of their fate when this life is done."

Listening to him speak a relief born smile lit Sally-May's face. The smile held the shadow of a small victory. He hadn't even considered the prospect of her holding anything back. He might know a lot but he didn't know everything.

"I think of the future a lot John," she said honestly. "I think of it all the time."

"My name is David."

Sally-May closed her eyes to the world around her. She tried to close her mind to the soft voice that kept repeating those four simple words. She prayed silently for the soft sound of the wheels on pavement to block it out. In a moment she was sound asleep.

*****

They dropped her very close to the building where her afternoon class was scheduled. Sally-May attended the lecture sitting at the back of the class her mind in a fog. The short nap in the car had not pushed away the memory, it had made it that much clearer.

"Can you please tell someone I'm here?"

He was a big man. He was stronger in spirit than any man or woman she had known. Three times she had been privileged to see the experiment and each time he had fought hard. Only when he had been pleading for her help had he seemed weak. Even then he had never broken down as a lot of other men might have. The prospect of a man being weak and admitting it to a woman hypnotized Sally-May to the point where a determined voice literally jerked her out of her revere.

"Earth calling Sally-May. The class is over."

Startled Sally-May looked up to find three friends standing beside her desk. One of these girls was Alice James her roommate. The others were Kathleen Smith and Helen Masterson, two girls who shared a room next to hers. Sally-May looked at the girls then around at the room and smiled.

"So it is. Goodness my head's in the clouds isn't it? I'd better get going."

She reached for her backpack but Alice stopped her.

"Sally can we talk to you?" Alice asked quietly.

"Surely," Sally said guardedly.

"This is going to sound like prying but we wouldn't say anything if we were worried about you," Alice said. "We're your friends."

Sally-May looked at the three faces standing above her and wondered at the almost magic use of the word friend. For a moment the three girls looked at each other as if wanting the other to begin. It was Kathleen who took the first step.

"Sally, you're losing weight and you weren't exactly chunky to begin with. You just don't look healthy," Kathleen said.

"Are you eating?" asked Helen. "I mean, if you have a money problem you can get some help at social services. They helped me out last winter remember?"

Sally-May shifted uncomfortably under their worried attentions. They were the only people she spoke to outside the church. They always seemed to be kind decent girls worthy of the name friend, but they just didn't understand.

"I guess I've been pretty busy what with ministering and all," she admitted. "But I have been eating. Truly."

Alice swallowed hard and stood with her mouth open for a long minute before speaking. Sally-May found herself not wanting to hear what this friend had to say.

"Sally far be it from me to get in between a person and their faith but what kind of religion kills you with over work?" Alice asked.

Trying hard not to look as if she were running away Sally-May gathered her things and stood. As she did this, her hands trembled with clearly broadcast discomfort. The whispered voice came back to her in all its strength.

"This thing they're doing to me. It doesn't have anything to do with religion Sally-May it's just torture and it's pointless."

"I appreciate your concern really I do. It's possible a little more balance is called for I promise you I will find that balance. I do know how to take care of myself. I have to go. I need to do some studying."

Half running from the three worried faces she left them behind. By the time she reached the street she was running full speed. She ran along a long narrow street drawing curious looks from students' teachers and simple passersby then up a tree lined path to her dormitory.

Sally-May climbed the stairs entered the room she shared with Alice James. She stood beside her bed wavering slightly on rubber muscled legs. Her side of this room was spotlessly neat. The other half while not exactly messy was much more relaxed. She had always thought that Alice's inability to maintain her side of the room properly showed a slight lack of character. Now she wondered was this spotless half a room really more about control than cleanliness?

Again the voice of the man locked in the small prison echoed in her mind.

"This thing they're doing to me. It's going to kill me. It doesn't have anything to do with religion Sally-May it's just torture and it's pointless."

Sally-May let her backpack full of books slip from her shoulders. It hung from one hand for a full minute then she let it fall to the floor. Looking down at the bag Sally-may saw in her mind's eye everything she had ever believed. She saw it from a point distant and disconnected. She saw it all and she felt doubt.

Could any human construction have the power to bridge the gap between earth and heaven? Where was heaven? Was it in another diminution, on another planet? Was it a reality so different that human physics could not even recognize it as a place?

Quietly Sally-May began to cry. She cried out tears of bitterness born of a lifetime of grief. She mourned for a sister's unjust death and a mother so trapped in her life the most she could do was insure her one remaining child leave and not return. She even mourned for her father who in some distant past had become convinced that control violence and blind duty were a substitute for love.

In her mind she saw herself in a boat on a stream. She was young, a very young Sally-May crying out for a paddle to steer her way to shore. A paddle appeared in her hands. It was a paddle full of holes.

Her legs lost what strength they had left and she lowered herself to her knees. In a stunned wave of shock she realized that she could not pray. She no longer knew if there was anyone listening.

*****

The girls arrived at the dormitory just in time for supper. An hour later Alice breezed into her shared room.

"You going to miss supper Sally. You better hurry. The chicken's gone, all they have left is fish and something nasty looking with tofu."

Sally-May lay huddled in a lump on the floor.

"Sally?"

Alice laid a hand on her friend's shoulder and learned nothing but the fact that the girl was alive. She rolled her over and was immediately shocked into running to the room next door where her two friends shared space.

"Big trouble I need you now!" she called.

At first glimpse of the girl on the floor Helen dropped to her knees and began to examine her. She took her pulse monitored her respiration and pinched the tendon at the back of her ankle to see her response to sudden pain. The girl on the floor seemed oblivious to it all.

Looking up at her friends Helen said, "OK, this is only two years of pre-med and five years as a candy striper talking but she looks catatonic. Our little saint has either lost her halo big time and scored herself some drugs or she's had some kind of a breakdown."

"Shit," exclaimed Alice. "I knew we should have talked to her before this!"

Alice picked up the phone and began to dial for an ambulance. Kathleen, hovering by the door, spoke up seeing a way to be of help.

She said, "Well if we can't ace the intervention we can handle the rescue. I'll go out front and wait for the ambulance."

Alice gave the voice on the other end of the phone line the directions and an explanation of what was happening. She was assured that an ambulance would be there very soon. By the time she had hung up the phone Helen had

119

taken the blankets off Sally-May's bed and was covering her up. Helen looked up to find Alice watching her, a question in her eyes.

"This is all we can do keep her warm," Helen said. "I wonder if we should phone that guy of hers? God what's his name? John Hugh that's it!"

Alice gave a rough ironic laugh. She had seen more than enough of John Hugh to want to keep him at a good distance. She liked men who expected obedience and submission out of a woman, as much as she liked a tooth in need of a root canal.

"You want to call that fire and brimstone preacher? Hell no! I wouldn't be surprised if mixed feelings over him might have brought this crap on. She's got a brilliant mind but it's balanced on the top of an emotional sand castle."

"Bad home life?" Helen asked.

"I've heard worse but hers was pretty nasty. Mind you that's just the stuff I know. She's constantly almost but not quite about to tell me something but I've never been able to get it out of her. I don't know, maybe she'll tell the doctor. She probably better."

In the silence after this last comment both young women heard Kathleen coming down the hall directions to someone. Behind this was the unmistakable squeaking clatter of a stretcher. Along with that came the murmuring of female voices commenting on this shocking piece of excitement. Nothing happened in this house full of women that was not talked over in detail. The crowd would be dissecting this event for months.

Alice picked up Sally-May's backpack put it neatly on her desk then got out of the way. Their friend needed help and they were seeing that she got it. What would happen after that would be up to her.

CHAPTER 16

Kevin St. John looked at the woman sitting across from him. His stomach did a lurching jump as if he had just ridden an express elevator from the top floor of a skyscraper all the way down to the basement. He took a deep breath and put the burger in his hands down. The fast answer to this strange statement was unlikely, far to unlikely, yet he could not help himself.

"When did you see a man with a tattoo like this?" he asked.

She gave a slight smile shrinking under his suddenly stern attitude. He tried to relax a bit so she would relax but it was hard, damn hard.

"A while ago," she said vaguely. "It's kind of a long story."

"I take it you're a nudist?" he asked.

"No I'm a novelist."

She smiled slightly as if she knew her answer to this question was completely incongruous. He smiled back at her and felt his free floating stomach slip back into place. It had to be some kind of strange coincidence. The world had enjoyed a recent resurgence of Celtic art and culture. As his own partner had pointed out it was entirely possible for more than one man to have the sort of tattoo David carried.

Kevin looked down at his tray and knew he no longer wanted his lunch. He took a bite of the burger anyway and chewed. There was no doubt in his mind that David was a prisoner. If he was going to have the energy to find him he shouldn't skip meals. Two bites later the woman, in the process of finishing up her own lunch, spoke again.

"Who are you looking for that has a tattoo like that?" she asked.

There was an edge to her voice that put Kevin's nerves on the alert. This time when he looked at her she met his gaze without shrinking. There was something determined about her that let him know she would have to be sure about him before she spoke.

"Interesting guess," he said. "You must write mysteries. I'm looking for my brother. He's agency too investigating local religious cults. He vanished some weeks ago. Headquarters has assumed that he's gone under cover which is something he did have permission to do if he got the chance. I don't think he did."

She looked around at the very crowded food court. She frowned in a way that made Kevin think of amateur sleuths on old television shows. They were the sorts of shows where the victim usually deserved what they got at least a little. The murderer was just a little sympathetic yet solving his or her problems in the worst possible way. The amateur detective was just a teeny bit smarter than the police and often had a homicide detective for a best friend.

"My name is Claire Anderson. I'm staying in town at the old hotel on Main Street," she began.

Kevin felt like holding his breath. He had made a connection, a totally unexpected connection. Yet it probably meant nothing.

"I'm headed there myself I have reservations," he said. "The place sounded a bit pricey for my expense account so I thought I'd stop and eat here first."

"Actually it's fairly reasonable but it's just as well you stopped," she said.

"Why?" he asked.

She stood shouldered her purse and picked up her tray.

"I'd rather not talk here, it's too crowded and what I have to say is frankly way too good to be ignored by anyone close enough to overhear," she said. "I'll tell you at the hotel. I'll be reading a book in the lobby in about an hour. We can talk in the coffee shop they have. It's much quieter and more private."

*****

Clare was trying to read. She was not succeeding. Clandestine meetings like this were infinitely easier to write about than to act out. On reflection she knew that the setting was far too much of a cliché. Real investigators simply did not meet like this.

A figure stepped out of the elevator. It was the man from the mall. Clearly he must have hurried here from the mall and checked in ahead of her picking this spot. She closed the book she'd been utterly failing to read and stood as he neared her spot.

Looking very business-like and official he took an identification wallet out of a pants pocket and showed her proof that he was with the FBI.

"All right Ms. Anderson my name is Kevin St. John. Can you please tell me what this is all about?"

Clare smiled and nodded toward the restaurant entrance. The place was almost empty, a perfect spot to talk.

"How about coffee and dessert? We can put it on my expense account," she said. "I can pretty much guarantee it's much bigger than yours."

He shook his head and pocketed his identification then pointed to the small couch she'd been sitting on. When he spoke a hard edge of impatience showed through. This was his business now and he would run the show.

"How about we sit right here and you tell me what you know," he said.

Claire shrugged then sat hugging the book suddenly feeling more than a little uncomfortable. He sat next to her, leaning on the low back of the couch facing her with strangely familiar blue eyes.

"Well, I'm waiting," he prodded.

Claire took a deep breath and let it out slowly. Putting a story like this in an e-mail was one thing. Saying it out loud to this deeply serious man was another.

"I once watched a man with a tattoo like that walk stark naked up my street in the middle of the night. It happened close to three or four weeks ago in Toronto Canada," she said simply.

"Shit."

Claire looked at Kevin St. John and wondered. His comment was not said with exasperation or disbelief. It was said in total unexpected shock. His face had gone very pale. Fumbling in a jacket pocket slightly he brought out a wallet.

As he did this he said, "Look this is against the rules, it's against every-thing. What I should do is take you in and get you to look through a bunch of pictures and see if you pick the right one. We don't have time for that, I have to know now."

He opened the wallet and flipped through several pictures. Finding what he was looking for he held it for Claire to see. It was her man. He was maybe two years younger here and clothed of course but there was no possibility of a mistake.

"That's him. This man is related to you isn't he?" she asked.

"He's my older brother David," he said. "We're both with the agency. I generally work computer crime. Officially I'm here physically tracing a hacker that's been a big pest to a bunch of different large companies. What I want to do is find my brother. Hopefully alive."

"Oh my," Claire said.

She struggled for something useful to say but nothing came to mind. Slowly the hand holding the wallet closed it up and moved to rest on Kevin St. John's lap. Claire looked up at his face. She saw a deep desperate hurt.

"You were brought here by an e-mail weren't you?" she asked.

"You wrote that?" he asked.

"Yes."

"Ms. Anderson..."

"Call me Claire," she said.

"All right Claire," he said. "I there anything connected to this that you didn't put in the e-mail?"

Claire thought of the pamphlet given to her by Mary-Ann. Then she thought of Sally-May. Could an innocent child like that really be a part of something that would hold and torture a man? Could her dedication to this faith of hers really make her that blind?

Claire stood and opened her purse. She took out the pamphlet and handed it to Kevin. He took it without a shred of understanding.

"What's this?" he asked.

Claire said, "You can read it while I drive. I think we need to go and talk to the chief of campus police. He'd be able to explain the official side of things in a bit more detail."

Kevin slipped his wallet back in its pocket and stood pamphlet in hand. His worry for his brother was back under control now. He studied her a crooked smile lighting his face.

"Letting me tag along for the ride are you Miss Marple?" he asked.

Feeling a touch of annoyance Claire answered him. Her voice was stern and commanded his complete attention and belief.

"I'm a fantasy writer Mr. St. John. Believe me I do not like the situation into which I have been put. However I am stuck in this town till next Monday when I am scheduled to give a lecture. True-life crime is not my genre however disappearing men defiantly qualify. I saw your brother appear then disappear twice. I swear to you that is the absolute truth. Now, shall we go?"

He shrugged and said, "Yes ma'am. Lead the way."

*****

Alice sat curled on her bed reading a history book. A small tap on the door pulled her out of her concentration slightly. She spoke without looking up.

"Come in."

John Hugh opened the door and stood looking into the room. Alice glanced up at him gave a half smile and looked down at her book.

"Where is Sally-May?" he asked.

"The moon."

He made an impatient frown.

"It was a simple question Alice," he said. "If you don't know you need not be rude."

Alice put a bookmark in the textbook she was reading and set it aside. She leaned against the wall her bed was set beside and crossed her arms looking up at the stiffly grim young preacher. This was the first time he had entered the building, which was designated as completely female. He looked as uncomfortable as if he had come upon her wrapped in nothing but a towel.

It was an attitude that had echoes of old fashioned gentlemanly behavior that Alice forced herself to admit had its attractions. When you combined them with his undeniable good looks she could see why Sally-May had been attracted to this man. At the same time the chauvinistic streak that went with this behavior was something that she personally could never tolerate.

"What are you doing here John?" she asked after letting him hover at the door for a moment.

"I have been trying to find Sally-May," he said, looking uncomfortable for the first time in her memory. "We were supposed to have supper before the prayer meeting. Is she doing extra school work?"

Feeling just a little stubborn Alice said, "I'm not sure I want to tell you."

Looking increasingly annoyed, almost human, his superior attitude came back twice as strong.

"Sally-May is my responsibility. I need to know where she is," he declared.

Alice said, "John, what you need is a mental enema. You're a guy she met in a prayer group, nothing more."

"Her immortal soul is in my care," he said firmly.

Alice launched herself off her bed and crossed the room to stand in front of the door. He took a half step away from her, which came close to angering her even more. It was as if she could infect him with sin simply by being close.

"If you're talking about caring about Sally-May then you dropped the damn ball," she growled.

The comment caught him off guard. He didn't understand and was letting it show. Alice knew she had the upper hand and she backed off letting him relax a little. She didn't have to overpower him like this. The truth was overpowering enough.

"What do you mean?" he asked.

"An ambulance took her away around supper time. I called the hospital to check up on her about ten minutes ago. They are not letting her have any visitors," she answered.

Gripping his bible with both hands he looked genuinely concerned. Mentally Alice gave him a couple of small points for sincerity. It didn't change her opinion of him in her mind much but it did make him just a little more three- dimensional.

"Alice, what are you talking about?" he asked. "Has there been an accident?"

For a moment the truth about what they were talking about made Alice more angry than victorious. Her roommate was no game piece to use to score a point against this idiot. She was sick and Alice was positive this man was key to her problems.

"She's had a nervous breakdown you stupid bible thumping moron," she said.

"I don't believe you," he said with such utter dismissal it had Alice fuming once again.

For a split second the real John Hugh had shown through. That John was a man who probably genuinely cared about the girl they were talking about. Unfortunately that second had passed. John Hugh fundamentalist preacher and full-fledged creep had come back in full force.

"You want to talk belief I'll tell you what I believe. I believe you and you're chauvinist pig friends pushed her into this. There's something about that cult of yours that's sick John Hugh. I think she figured out she should give the lot of you your walking papers. She couldn't do it so she had a breakdown instead."

John was silent for a long minute. He looked as if he heard every word she'd said and given her words a weight she did not understand. But if it came to that she really didn't understand this man at all. She only knew he was bad for Sally-May.

"She is in the hospital?" he asked.

"Yes," Alice said. "And don't bother trying to see her they won't let you. They said they wouldn't even let family see her at this stage. She needs a break. She needs a break from you."

Something behind the man's eyes went very hard and he said, "If you will excuse me, I have something I need to think about."

He turned and walked away from the door. Alice stepped out into the hall and watched John push through the door at the end of the hall. The short set of stars there would end at a door that was closest to a parking lot at the rear of the building.

For a short time in their conversation, the man had looked uncertain and worried for the first time. Trying not to think of the strange hard cast this uncertainty had transformed into Alice closed the door and went back to work.

CHAPTER 17

The hospital serving both the town and the surrounding rural population was called Mercy General. It was a large five-story structure capable of providing the many and varying needs of the surrounding population. The staff understood the population they served because for the most part they had come from the area.

Because of this Dorothy Hammond senior nurse on the evening shift faced the young man in front of her and knew exactly what sort of problem she was facing. She had been pulled from a patient's room by a cryptic page to face down this theatrically angry young man. Looking into his fiery indignant eyes she immediately understood the patient with whom she had just been talking.

"I'm very sorry Mr. Hugh, the doctor has left firm orders. No visitors," she said with carefully hidden enjoyment.

As she expected the man did not come close to backing down.

"You have no authority to keep me from that woman," he said.

John Hugh fumed as Dorothy picked Mary-Ann's patient record from the rack and reread the scant information that had to date been entered. She had a lot of extra training to handle the troubled patients that ended up on her ward. The biggest job however often involved dealing with the friends and families who didn't understand that the most important thing a troubled person needed was time out.

Her lips a thin line Dorothy looked up from clipboard in her hands. She'd only done this as a time filling ploy. He had to be taught that this was a playing field where he was not going to even be allowed into the game.

"Young man in the absence of a doctor or administrator I am in charge of this floor. I have every authority to kick you out of this hospital," she said calmly.

"I'm not leaving here till I see Sally-May," he said.

Dorothy looked toward a nurse at the floor's main desk. The nurse standing there rolled her eyes in exasperation then picked up the phone and stood waiting for instructions.

Giving her helper a quick glance skyward that had the woman smiling broadly Dorthy said, "Fran get security up here."

Turing back to John she said, "Mr. Hugh you are not a blood relation or a husband. You wouldn't get in to see her if you were but at least you'd have a reasonable basis for being angry. You are also making a nuisance of yourself. I want you to leave. Now."

"I am that woman's spiritual advisor. She does not need a doctor. The works of man do not but sin in the eyes of God," he intoned.

Genuinely angry now Dorothy slid the clipboard in her hand back into the rack. When she turned her attention back to John she found he had taken several steps toward the corridor. Her firm no nonsense voice stopped him in his tracks.

"Don't you bring God into this boy that's half that girls problem. I ought to know I've just spent the last hour listening to her talk. Now get your sorry ass off my floor before security gets here or I will be sorely tempted to have you charged with trespassing."

John Hugh stood fuming his strong frame trembled slightly. A large orderly pushing a cart full of equipment along the hall towards the central nurses' station pushed his cart to the wall then stood blocking the way. John looked in his direction as if sizing him up. The man smiled and shook his head.

"You got a good build there kid," he said. "The thing is I really don't think you know how to use those muscles of yours. Not the way you feel like doing right now. I worked in the state mental hospital for five years before this son. I don't care how big you are, try me and you'll end up in restraints with a criminal charge on your head."

John Hugh turned and walked to the nearby elevators. He pressed the button and waited a long uncomfortable time till the doors opened and he was able to escape.

130

*****

John Huge sat alone in the van eyes on the parking lot entrance to the hospital. The sun was setting. The prayer meeting he normally would have led this evening would be braking up, having been led by one of his seconds.

"Don't you bring God into this boy that's half that girls problem."

He had to know what was really wrong. Alice, this nurse, they both claimed his woman's faith had taken her to this extreme. Was this a crisis of faith? He needed to get to Sally-May to make sure she came back to the proper path.

The large confident orderly came out of the door and walked to a car nearby then drove off. John watched the car disappear down the road. A man with God on his side had little to fear but discretion was not an ungodly quality. John slipped out of the van locked the door. Making sure no one was watching he entered the hospital by the same door.

The stairwell was dimly lit and very quiet. Feeling the slightest sound echo up through the floors as he went John climbed the stairs to the fourth floor. He slipped into the hall praying silently for guidance.

Moving carefully, very aware of the voices that echoed down the hall from the nurse's station John chose a door. This room held two men, one curled up in a ball possibly asleep the other watching a small television.

John turned the other way. He walked past a hand full of open doors then picked one that was closed. This room held two beds. One was empty, the other held a still and silent Sally-May. John slipped into the room carefully closing the door.

He approached the bed and stood waiting to be recognized. She lay silent, her head turned toward the window, her eyes open but seemingly unseeing. He made a soft sound in the back of his throat and her head turned in his direction. Still she said nothing.

"Sister what ails you?" he asked quietly.

Her voice was soft and faint as if her mind were coming back from a far-away place.

"I'm not your sister. I'm not anyone's sister anymore my sister is dead. I think my father killed her and dropped her body down the outhouse pit. You couldn't prove it without moving the cherry tree. How would I get anyone to move a whole tree?"

John frowned completely lost.

"Sister what are you saying?" he asked.

In a tone of voice he had never heard from her she barked, "I'm not your sister!"

Nerves jumping badly John glanced toward the closed door. Her voice had gone from whisper soft to loud enough to attract the attention of anyone who might be standing near the door. When he looked back at the woman in the bed quiet tears had begun to fall washing her cheeks in thin lines.

"All right Sally-May. I understand. Hush now or they'll come and make me go away," he said. "Why are you here?"

Again she gave him an answer that seemingly had nothing to do with the question.

"His name is David. Did you know that John? His name is David. He is brave and strong and we've been torturing him. It's wrong John."

John looked at the woman he thought he knew and felt a rush of anger and fear. He felt his hands begin to twitch slightly and he wished he had brought his bible. The big leather bound book was like a talisman against evil uncertainty.

Fishing for words Johns said, "It is for the greater good Sally-May. God sent him to us to pave the way."

He waited for the usual rout answer of "blessed be" and a calm look of acceptance. Instead she looked earnest, impassioned.

She said, "John tell me. Tell me how a thing made by man could reach heaven. Tell me you love me."

John opened his mouth completely at a loss. He took Sally-May's hand and held it tight.

"Of course I love you. That's why I'm here. I don't want you to fall back into sin."

The built up tension in Sally-May's body seemed to slowly drain out. She looked up at him, smiled slightly then her worry seemed to return.

"Why would we need these bodies to get to heaven?" she asked. "We leave our bodies behind to get there. You've got to stop it John. You have to tell them to let him go!"

John looked down at the woman in the bed and saw someone new. There was a strength there. He had seen it in the faces of women who refused to obey their husbands completely. He had seen the look in women who lusted after men without benefit of vows, who refused to believe men had the god given right to rule over women, who left husbands simply because the husband obeyed the bible and beat them to keep them in line.

"You need to correct your thoughts Sally-May," he said with a firmness he had never before needed.

She didn't seem to hear him. She didn't know how far away her thoughts were from the truth. She was his and he was losing her.

"John we need to save him," she continued earnestly. "We need to get help."

John felt his heart thump hard in his chest. Trying to move without thinking John casually went to the other bed and picked up the pillow. He loved her. He loved her too much to allow her to go to hell.

"You do agree with me don't you John?" she asked.

"I want you to go to heaven Sally-May," he said, knowing that the love had slipped back into his voice.

She smiled softly, knowingly, like a mother, like his mother. It made it so much easier.

"I know I will John. In my time. I'll see my mother and my sister. I won't have to worry ever again."

John drew very close to her bed holding the pillow in two hands.

"I know. Neither will I."

*****

Claire drove Kevin St. John to the university campus answering his questions as they went and learning a lot about the missing David St. John. Once they reached the campus Claire tried to lead the way to the building where Jim Young had his office.

"I could have sworn it was this way," Claire said faintly.

"Maybe I should have brought my boy scout compass?"

Claire stuck her tongue out at the FBI agent eliciting a friendly eruption of laughter. Claire smothered her own laughter as she regained her sense of direction and started walking again.

As they began to move again she said, "I was only there once kindly cut me some slack. When I write I can work it so my characters get where they need to be, reality takes a little more work."

Kevin frowned slightly and said, "Think you can write me a happy ending for this thing?"

Claire shrugged slightly and said, "I'm sorry. I know it's your brother but I think we both know in a case like this you need to hope for the best and prepare for the worst."

"Yeah you're right," Kevin said grimly. "I just hope this campus cop believes your story. If I'm going to have even half a chance of getting David back alive I'm going to need some professional help."

Once they found the office they were told that the chief was out investigating a robbery at one of the dorms and would be back momentarily. An hour and a half later he walked in. He gave her a wide smile at the same time throwing a sharp glance toward Kevin.

"Claire hello," he said as brightly as the hour allowed. "I didn't expect to see you again till Sunday night."

"Something's come up," Claire said.

"Is it important?" he asked. "It's been kind of a long day. I was about to leave for supper. My wife's visiting relation's up north daughters in tow so I'm on my own till Monday."

"All right then, we can talk in the restaurant," Claire said. "My treat."

Jim frowned and said, "Claire what's going on? Who's your friend?"

Kevin St. John pulled his identification out and held it so Jim could read the name on the badge. His brows raised just slightly and Claire knew he had made a connection with his other visitor.

He said, "Give me ten minutes and we'll go."

The trio walked a handful of blocks to a small Italian restaurant where Kevin and Claire talked and Jim listened. They were drinking coffee and finishing up desert as Jim rolled the facts as they had presented them around in his head.

He said, "Damn this is difficult. Kevin are you sure you believe what our literary friend is saying?"

Kevin smiled and nodded.

"Like I said we checked it out and as strange as they are the dogma that The Power and The Blood spews out fits the facts. I think they might be holding my brother at that retreat of theirs. Back when he first failed to show after his trip down here our office phoned to see if he had checked out of his hotel. He was booked into a place close to the highway. Supposedly he had checked out. Problem is when they were pressed for details they couldn't remember if he had personally checked out or just dropped his keys into the bin they have."

Nodding his understanding Jim followed this logic to its conciliation.

"So they could have grabbed him then went to his hotel and checked him out in a way that no one would actually remember seeing him," he said.

Claire listened to this in her mind a vivid picture of David St. John, battered and weak. It made her more than a little impatient with these careful lawmen.

She asked, "Can't you just get a search warrant or something and go up there?"

Both men were a picture of understanding and frustration.

"You have to show probable cause," said Jim. "Cop shows notwithstanding Claire getting a search warrant is actually a time consuming business."

Kevin added, "FBI or ordinary cop the rules are pretty much the same. You have to prove to a judge that you have a good reason to violate the sanctity of someone's home or property."

Jim's cell phone rang and he answered. To Claire he looked like a tired man who was suddenly picturing his bedtime vanishing into the distance.

He said, "Aw hell that's all we need. Yeah I'd like to, thanks for calling. I have someone else here who would have an interest I'll bring him along."

Looking grim he stowed his phone away.

Kevin asked, "What's up?"

"That was the sheriff he's at the hospital," Jim explained. "He says we have a dead student on our hands."

"Why would I be interested? I assume you were referring to me?" Kevin asked.

Jim sighed and pushed his cup toward the center of the table.

He explained, "Technically I was talking about both of you. One of our students a Sally-May Le Blank was taken to the hospital this afternoon suffering an emotional brake down. A half hour ago she was found by one of the nurses, dead."

Claire felt her face go white.

"Was it suicide?" she asked.

Jim shook his head sadly.

"Nothing so neat and tidy. The on call resident took one look at the body and called the sheriff. According to the bruising around the girl's mouth and nose this was very defiantly murder."

CHAPTER 18

When they arrived at the hospital they found a scene that was both quiet, and at the same time radiated a kind of involved intensity. Vividly aware of where they were everyone involved seemed to go about his or her business trying hard to not disturb the other patients.

The actions of each of the evidence gathering professional fit together like the piece of a puzzle that made a fascinating scene. In Claire's mind it all belonged on a television screen. To see it in real life in the service of this girl she had tried to help was just so wrong. Emotionally lost young girls did not get murdered, they found their way, bid the cult that had temporarily given them mental shelter goodbye and went on with their lives.

After confirming that this was the same Sally-May she had talked to in the mall Claire backed away. A short time later Kevin and Jim found her in the floor's common room. She had already worked her way through some vending machine hot chocolate. At this point for lack of a better thing to do her hands were playing with the empty cup.

"They've taken her down stairs to the morgue," Jim said.

Kevin cocked a thumb in the direction of the corridor. His face held a puzzled expression accented by a half smile.

"You backed away pretty fast. I expected you to be hovering, taking notes and asking technical questions," he commented.

Well settled in an armchair Claire shook her head and suppressed a shiver.

"I don't know," she said setting the cup in her hands on a table. "It's a bit too real for me right now. I mean I talked to that girl. I tried to help her. Anyway I can't think when I'd use the information. I've used murders and crime scenes and stuff before but not in a way where I'd need any detail. I'm not a mystery writer. I just don't think that way."

Lips drawn into a crooked smile at this Kevin fell into a seat on a couch. Claire turned toward him and smiled waiting for the question she could see in his eyes.

"Why don't you just write a mystery for a change?" he asked.

She rolled her eyes at the innocent and very common question. Both men immediately looked both interested and confused. Like most who worked in disciplines strictly set in the real world they simply didn't understand.

"Some writers can write in any genre that suits their needs they get an idea they work with it no matter what the type of story. That's not the way my brain works. I do have one that's close; it's a murder mystery with a ghost in it. The ghost solves the murder."

Still hovering in the center of the room Jim shoved his hands deep into his pants pockets. One hand pulled out some change. He went to stand in front of the vending machine and contemplate his choices.

Counting the coins he said, "It'd be nice if you could get that kind of help in real life. What would stop you doing the same thing only having some real live person doing the sleuthing?"

Grateful for the distraction from why they were here in the first place Claire gave the question some thought. It was a hard question to answer particularly when speaking to men who were used to the routine practice of learning a skill then practicing that skill. How did you explain to that sort of person that with writing sometimes there's something more?

"Like I said some fiction writers, quite a few really, can write whatever they want or need. Even that sort of writer does tend to have a sort of thing they prefer to work on. There's a writer's exercise that illustrates what I'm talking about. You start with several different writers know for writing several different types of genre. You give them a scenario of a man walking down the street, and see what you get."

Jim dropped some change into the common room coffee machine and a black brew began filling a cup. He stood watching the machine work then took the cup and sipped the result wincing slightly.

"So, what do you get?" he asked.

"The horror writer has a monster hand come out of a sewer grate. The romance writer has a beautiful woman cross the man's path. Me, I'd likely have him turn a corner and end up somewhere completely unreal but have it turn out that he should have been there all along."

Claire could see an idea form in Kevin's eyes. It was clear he'd made a kind of mental connection. Claire waited for him to organize his thoughts and speak.

He said, "You're starting to sound like a criminal who pulls a bank job or con, or some other kind of crime the same way every time even though he knows eventually it's going to get him caught. Are you saying you can't write a straight crime story?"

Claire shrugged and said, "I don't really want to. I'd only end up bored and miserable. If I'm going to spend time being bored and miserable I might as well go back to answering phones for a living. I have ten novels sitting on my computer back home. The screen adaptation of the third book is in pre-production as we speak. It paid off my house."

Kevin raised his hands.

"All right I surrender. I refuse to mess with success," he said playfully.

Sheriff Nate Kranston entered the common room. He held a small open notebook in his hands. John perched on the arm of a chair and the three people waiting in the lounge sat silent giving him the floor.

"I have an address for our Mr. John Hugh. I'm having him brought in for questioning. I assume you gentlemen will want to watch?" Nate asked.

"Defiantly," said Kevin. "This is your case sheriff but this girl's death, may be connected to the disappearance of a federal agent who also happens to be my brother. I'd appreciate all the help you can give."

Kranston tapped his notebook in his hands twice then shoved it in his pocket. When he spoke he was clearly a little embarrassed. He was a big man who looked as much a part of the territory he policed as the rocks and trees on its hillsides. The sharp eyes lighting his weathered face betrayed the presence of an equally sharp and practical mind.

"Let's be above board here shall we?" he said.

"Of course," said Kevin.

The Sheriff scratched a stubble-covered cheek and glanced back the way he had come as if wanting to avoid being overheard by any of his people.

"A lot of men in my situation would resent being hovered over by a Fed. and a Yanky cop. I'm not one of them. My people know what they're doing but I have to face the fact that we don't have murders here very often. When we do it's generally a lot more obvious. I'd appreciate all the experienced help I can get."

Claire stood and shouldered her purse.

"Well shall we go?" she said.

"Hold on a bit miss..."

Kevin quickly stood and stepped between Claire and the sheriff.

"I can't explain sheriff," said Kevin. "You wouldn't believe me if I tried. Miss Anderson is connected to my brother's disappearance. There's an outside possibility that she may be of some help if she comes along."

Kranston thought for a moment then sighed and said,

"All right, if you insist. Just promise me one thing."

"Name it first," said Kevin.

"There's something going on here that you don't want to tell me involving this woman. I can handle that this murder is enough for my plate. Promise me that if it effects my case or any of the people I am sworn to protect then I get to know."

"Sheriff," Kevin said. "I promise you if you need to know then you will."

Nate sighed, his eyes bouncing from Kevin to Claire to John Young.

"I can accept that," he said. "Let's go."

They had traveled from the restaurant to the hospital with Claire following Jim Young's car. They now repeated the process with Jim in turn followed the sheriff.

"I feel like I'm on parade," Claire said.

"It's getting a bit late. You know the odds of this having anything to do with my brother even if the cult does have him are pretty slim. You could probably just drop me off and go back to the hotel. I'm sure Jim would drive me back."

Claire smiled. It was a half-hearted try at getting her to back away from the situation but she wasn't going to take the bait. She might not be a crime writer but this was a chance to experience something under normal circumstances she would never get near. She wasn't giving up this chance without a fight.

She said, "I'm sure he would too but I want to be here anyway. Call it a morbid obsession with plot. I just have to find out what happens."

At the police station Claire Kevin and Jim were ushered into a small dark room where a uniformed officer was operating a camera. On the other side of a one way mirror was a small room with a table and three chairs. A few minutes of quiet waiting rewarded them with a view of John Hugh being ushered into the room by sheriff. A uniformed officer with a tape recorder sat at the desk and immediately began recording.

"Please sit Mr. Hugh," said sheriff Kranston. "I understand you're upset but there are a few things we have to talk over before I can have my man drive you home."

"I understand," said John.

"Okay just for the record please state your name and occupation," Nate began.

"My name is John Hugh," John said mechanically. "I work part time as a carpenter's helper. I am also a senior student at the university in town and a preacher."

Leaning on the table John Hugh was fingering one of the bracelets he wore nervously. It was clear from his next question that the sheriff had noticed it as well.

"You preach for the group calling itself The Power and the Blood?" he said.

"I do." John said.

"Sally-May belonged to the same group?"

"She did," John answered. "I brought her into the fold myself."

The statement was delivered with a noticeable amount of pride. A thought went through Claire's head about pride being one of the seven deadly sins. Then she thought again. Pride was likely the least of this man's sins.

"Why were you so insistent on seeing her this evening?" Nate asked changing the subject just slightly.

John Hugh stared into space for a long moment. He jerked very slightly as if he suddenly realized that he had forgotten where he was then answered.

"I...I was worried for her," he said.

"The head nurse for that floor describes you as being very impassioned," the Sheriff prodded gently.

John fumbled for words for a moment then said, "We have, had, a relationship."

"Were you lovers?"

The lost look in John's eyes faded and he sat a little taller in his chair. This was clearly a subject with which he felt comfortable.

"Not in the way of the body," he explained. "We had an understanding though that our future paths were parallel."

"You wanted to marry?"

John frowned slightly and said, "I never proposed. Sally-May was preoccupied with her studies and that would have interfered with her duties as a wife."

Watching this from the other side of the two-way mirror Claire crossed her arms and scowled. She glanced toward Jim and Kevin who seemed to be waiting for a reaction from her. She stuck her tongue out at them. Both men laughed and even the male officer handling the video camera stifled a smile.

Claire returned her attention to the interrogation room. This room was completely separate from that and she'd already been told they could not be heard. But editorializing seemed so inappropriate in the face of this oddly mundane drama. They were here because someone was dead.

"You should come first," said the sheriff.

John Hugh seemed increasingly confident. When he answered this comment he seemed almost comfortable with his surroundings. Claire smiled at the skillful way the Sheriff had created this comfort. Comfortable men so often said far too much.

"It is a man's duty to dominate his woman. He should be her concern not the world. I am a patient man. However, I knew that Sally-May would finish school and learn her proper place in time."

Nate asked, "What did you do after the nurse insisted you leave?"

"I went out and sat in my van for a time. I admit I was angry," John frowned and a shadow touched his eyes.

When he spoke again Claire knew he was lying.

"Eventually I calmed down and realized she was simply obeying the orders of the man to which she answered. After that I went home."

"Actually I believe the psychiatry resident for the hospital is a woman," Nate said, sounding slightly smug.

A slight frown touched John Hugh's mouth. A pointed comment seemed to float there for a moment then it drifted away unsaid.

"My mistake," he muttered.

"While you were sitting in the parking lot did you see anyone hanging around?" Nate asked.

"I did not," John answered, sounding slightly defensive. "I was worried for Sally-May and not particularly interested in my surroundings."

Startling John Hugh slightly Sheriff Kranston stood and waved a large expansive hand toward the door. Following his example John also stood. The officer that was operating the audio tape recorder stayed sitting. He did not turn off the machine.

"All right Mr. Hugh that will be all for now. You understand that we will probably want to talk to you at least once or twice more?"

"Yes of course," John said. "I wish to help any way I can."

Kranston led John out of the interrogation room. Both the officer in the room with the tape recorder and the officer operating the camera turned their tools off almost at once.

A few moments later the sheriff entered. His mouth was thin and his face pinched as if he had been chewing on tin foil.

He said, "That boy is as guilty as sin. All we have to do is find the evidence."

Both Jim and Kevin clearly agreed.

"What happens next?" asked Claire.

"What happens next dear lady," said Kevin. "Is we all go to our respective beds and get some sleep."

He gave her a wide smile and wrapped her right arm around his left then escorted her out into the hall. Looking both tired and amused Jim and sheriff Kranston followed.

The sheriff said, "Miss Anderson, in the movies you can catch a murderer in about ninety minutes. On TV they only take an hour. In real life even if you're pretty sure you know who did it, the same result can take a whole lot longer."

CHAPTER 19

John Hugh shared a small two-bedroom apartment with three other cult seniors; Martin Brown, Logan Smith and Aaron Combs. When the police dropped him off well after midnight he entered quietly expecting them to be asleep and the apartment dark. Instead he locked the apartment's door and looked along the short hallway to see the kitchen light on. He was pondering whether he had the energy to go and turn the light off when the voice of Martin Brown drew him into the light.

"John? Where have you been all this time? You missed the evening meeting. I was forced to substitute for you."

John looked at his roommates then down at the keys in his hands. They were sitting on kitchen chairs waiting for him to speak. Empty mugs sat on the table surrounding a large pot of herbal tea. Faintly grasping for words he knew the basic truth was almost good enough.

He said, "Sally-May is dead. The police think she was murdered."

The room was silent for a full thirty seconds. Then the reality of this announcement began to transform itself into emotion. These men all knew and above all approved of Sally-May in spite of her unwomanly preoccupation with her education.

"Who in the world would murder Sally-May?" asked Martin. "The girl is an innocent!"

John slowly sank into a kitchen chair. With immense relief he understood faintly that it didn't matter if he betrayed his feelings in front of these people. They knew how he felt about Sally-May. They would assume his feelings would be for his loss, not for the vivid memory of holding a pillow over a limply struggling woman's face. It had happen so fast, so very fast.

He said, "I don't know who would want to murder her. All I know is an ambulance took her to the hospital early this evening and now she's dead."

Logan Smith, a stocky young man studying politics and religion took up the questioning. John began to feel as if he had not left the interrogation room at the police station. Fate had simply walked him from one set of questioners to another.

"Why was she at the hospital in the first place?" Logan asked.

"The doctor labeled it a nervous breakdown. They wouldn't let me in to see her openly so I slipped in after visiting hours. I spoke to her and learned the truth. What she really suffered was a crisis of faith. She begged me to call the police about the Blessed one and help free him. I spoke to her firmly about regaining her faith then came home from the hospital. No one was here. A short time later a squad car came to take me to the police station. They wanted to talk to me about who might have done this."

"Heaven help the weakness of a woman," Aaron muttered.

John eyed him confused. There was a tone in his voice he did not understand. It was subtle but it was there.

"Did you see no one around that might be the killer?" Logan asked.

John jumped up from his chair and leaned against a kitchen counter. For a moment he looked and felt trapped. He knew it and he also knew it was the wrong image to project. It took very little effort to transform that trapped feeling to one of anger. Staring at his own face reflected in the kitchen window he said;

"I don't believe it was murder. I think they gave her some sort of mind drug to calm her nerves and it killed her. This murder story is just to absolve the hospital of guilt."

Martin stood and said, "John I think you should get some sleep. You've had a hard night. A little rest will help you think more clearly."

Numbly grateful for the tactful dismissal John nodded. Without further comment he turned and left the kitchen. Alone in his room he closed the door and fell on the bed fully clothed. In thirty seconds he was sound asleep.

*****

Aaron moved to speak but Martin waved him silent. A moment later the three men heard the bedroom door close. When it was closed Aaron spoke.

146

"I don't want to say this of a brother but not even a small town police force would mistake an accidental drug fatality for murder. Why would he think such a thing?"

"I will say just this," said Martin. "The sheriff is a local man but he's no fool. The county cornier is the head surgeon for that hospital. I know for a fact he's a Harvard man and more than sharp enough to tell a drug over dose from murder."

The two men locked eyes. Aaron's eyes widened slightly in understanding and Martin nodded.

"Pass the word," Martin said. "Someone stays with him at all times."

"Martin what are you saying here?" asked Logan.

Martin's answer was sharp and uncompromising.

"For a moment I am saying exactly that and no more. Our brother needs emotional support. Elaborate unnecessarily and you will be liable for censure do you understand?"

Aaron Combs, physics doctoral candidate and key technician for the sacrifice stood and took his empty mug to the sink. He put it in the sink then leaned against the counter looking out at the dark night. He had long ago rationalized the treatment of his experimental subject as evil done in the name of a greater good. The idea that this evil might someday be discovered by the outside world was a thought he had never allowed himself. They were in the right and as such would succeed. Nothing could be allowed to stand in the way of that success.

"The experiment is to be held again tomorrow. If we are to eventually succeed in reaching the dimensional existence we are searching for we must continue our patterning of the computer program controlling the transmitter. It learns a little more every time."

Martin said, "I am going to speak with the master. I will drive to the sanctuary now, tonight. We'll speak after morning prayers."

Martin crossed the kitchen to the hall he stopped and looked back when Aaron spoke again. He had turned from the window and was leaning against the sink, arms crossed. "Remind the Master this encumbrance can easily be removed from our shoulders. We've talked over problems like this in theory in preparation for possible threat. I confess I never thought the preparations would be necessary but the Master had more wisdom than I."

Martin nodded slightly and said, "I will do so."

Logan spoke up uncertainly.

"Is there something I'm missing here?" he asked.

"Yes there is," said Martin firmly. "And I would advise that this ignorance continue. For your own good."

*****

At one time the Master ran a profitable mining company. Then he progressed to a series of even more profitable investments which brought him a huge fortune. In his old age he now left the cult's enclosure only to walk in the woods. Taking one look at Martins' tired and grim face as the younger man requested a private audience the master nodded and suggested a walk. He did not speak till they were far away from even an accidental ear.

"Do you truly believe this of our brother?" the Master asked. "Do you believe he has killed sister Sally-May?"

Martin nodded reluctantly and said, "I even think he had good reason. He claims Sally-May suffered a crisis in faith. She wanted to tell the police about the blessed one. The world would not understand if this man was found in our care."

The Master walked a few yards further then stopped and rested his right hand on the trunk of a thick-bodied lodge pole pine. He studied the pattern of the bark and followed it up into the sky. From the sky his eyes drifted down to the ground.

"You're right. This problem must be taken care of with dispatch. The police are not fools. They have ways of learning the truth and they will pick Brother John up again, likely within forty eight hours. It is possible they will simply question him again. In the end lacking any other suspect they will pick him up and charge him. Once that happens he will be completely beyond us."

"John's loyalty has never been in question," Martin said. "He will not speak of his reason for the crime."

"He may not mean to break faith with us, yet the police have ways of questioning men and having them talk even without their own intentions," the Master said.

Martin rubbed a hand over his face and scratched his stubble covered chin.

"Aaron read the truth in what John said as well and agreed with me, though we said nothing out loud. He told me to remind you of matters you two have discussed in private. He did not tell them to me he simply assumed you would remember."

The master contemplated this statement. He smiled sadly. For a fleeting moment to Martin he looked old, very, very old.

He said, "I understand and agree. Our brother will be the first of our number to experience the transportation. We will send him to heaven."

Martin's mouth fell open.

"Do we actually know how to do that? How many will go the first night?"

The Master turned and began to lead Martin back toward the main gate. A chipmunk scurried across their path. Through the trees both men saw a doe watch them for a long second then bound off through the green tinted shade.

"Only one will be sent Martin. He will not go man alive but he will go to heaven."

*****

Claire slept late the next morning and had breakfast brought up to her room. After ninety minutes worth of listlessly pecking at her lap top computer, trying to work a faint idea she had into a plot for a new book, she decided to go for a walk. There were far too many distractions here for work. That made the issue of filling time a bit uncomfortable.

It was Friday. She had nothing official to do till Sunday evening. At this point however the real reason she had come to this small town was eclipsed in her mind by the drama of the missing David St. John. The reality of the situation had been driven home the day before by look of quiet desperation in Kevin St. John's eyes. Making the situation all the sadder had been the sight of the lifeless body of Sally-May.

Crossing the hotel's small lobby Claire looked into the restaurant. It was just after eleven. Kevin St. John was sitting with a lunch time salad in front of him. He looked far from hungry. She entered the half-empty room and sat down in front of him without asking permission.

"One usually bites and chews at this point," she said.

Kevin looked down at his lunch then dropped his fork at the side of the bowl. Clearly this lunch was going to be a sad and largely neglectful end to some very nice greenery.

"Nice hint," Kevin said. "I'll take it under advisement."

"If you were a character in one of my books I'd say you felt trapped," Claire observed.

He gave a small smile and nodded.

"Perceptive of you," he said. "I've been trying to think up legal ways to get onto the grounds of that retreat. I'm not getting very far."

Not for the first time since she began this trip Claire pondered the difference between reality and fiction.

"You think David is there," she asked.

Kevin leaned over his lunch elbows on the table.

"Unless they have some other more secret location it's the only place he could be that makes sense. Provided he's still alive. It's been a long time since you saw him in that parking lot. Over and above any signs of abuse just being zapped through the either one to many times could kill him."

They sat in silence for a time. Around them people entered the restaurant. They chatted with each other and the staff and when the food was brought they ate.

"Reality sucks," Claire said.

Her companion looked up from his salad brows raised.

"Pardon?" he asked.

"If this were one of my books you and Jim would sneak up there tonight break in carry him away. After a suitably exciting chase scene the whole lot of them would be arrested in by a squadron of FBI agents in battle gear," she said.

Claire paused in mid thought and smiled. She waved the idea away. As fantasy solutions to this problem went technicalities demanded a rewrite.

She said, "No that doesn't quite work. I think Navy intelligence would probably make more sense. After all they started this whole thing with that damn experiment of theirs."

Kevin gave a half smile.

"Hold that thought. The agency is so gun shy these days about cults and large actions sneaking in on our own is something we might have to do. Or I will. I'm not sure about navy intelligence backing us up though. No matter how responsible they might be technically."

For a moment he looked as if she had held up the shadow of an unconsidered hope. Claire waited for him to speak wondering what he was thinking about.

He mused, "Navy intelligence, if they knew someone had actually managed to get their classified accidental discovery to work they'd move in on the compound and confiscate any relevant equipment. That would get David out, although they'd probably put him under wraps till they finished examining him. I could handle that at least he'd be safe."

Claire thought this over and reluctantly shook her head. Even magical rescues had rules and this one had some dandies. Not the least of which was the fifty plus years between the original experiment and the present day.

"It'd take too long," she said.

"What do you mean? How do you know?" he asked.

She said, "Side effect of being a writer, you think in three dimensions in any given scenario. Even impossible rescues have to have a logical development. With a problem like this one you'd probably have to have a pretty high security clearance just to get in to talk to someone who'd tell you anything more than the Philadelphia experiment never happened. Anyone else would just recite the party line. Or say it never happened and believe what they're saying."

The faint hope that had shown in Kevin St. John's eyes faded. Claire began to wish she hadn't spoke.

"You're right. Back to reality sucks. If we're lucky that guy they talked to last night will break down when they charge him for the murder. If he admits to David being on the grounds then we have an in."

He took a fork full of now limp greenery from his salad, bit and chewed. To Claire he looked very much like a cow who just learned where hamburgers come from.

"They'll talk to him again today?" she asked.

Kevin swallowed shaking his head.

"To soon. The sheriff will probably make him swing a bit let him think he's off the hook. Also they have to wait till the preliminary lab work is done. After that we'll see."

CHAPTER 20

Sheriff Nate Kranston looked up from the paperwork on his desk to watch Bill Campbell, his chief deputy, enter the small office. He had a file folder in his hands. Nate held out a hand to receive the folder.

"I don't know what kind of preacher our boy might be but as a criminal he sucks big time," Bill said expansively as he handed the file over.

Leaving it closed Nate dropped the folder in the center of his desk. He leaned back in his chair right hand playing with the pen he'd been using. The other hand adjusted the folder so he could read the label. It read preliminary report. Such was the fate of an entire life to be boiled down to two words.

"And precisely what brand of idiocy are we referring to?" Nate asked.

"He left a print on the inside of the door, a possible on the door knob, though that was blurred when the nurse went in and out after discovering the body. There were several clear ones over on the bed. We've bagged the top pillow from the other bed and sent it to the lab up state for DNA testing. If it has her DNA on it and his we'll have him wrapped up. Just in case we also bagged the other pillows if we have the wrong one. They're in evidence."

Nate nodded his understanding then recited the scenario his deputy was suggesting. As a story it didn't take much inventing. Sadly the ending was the same no matter how you got there.

"So our boy insists on seeing his girl. They say no. He leaves then later sneaks in."

"An innocent enough act of misbehavior. It's even therapeutic if you bring a nice present," Bill said, adding. "Of course if the girl you sneak in to visit ends up dead that's another thing altogether."

Nate nodded his agreement and continued his observations. He would read the written report in due time but he had always preferred talking difficult situations out first. To him it was a thing that made dead words live.

"From what the head nurse says she was having a crisis in faith and about to leave the group. She even said something about wanting to talk to the police but the woman couldn't understand why. We'll have to talk to her again about that bit get her to go over it word for word as closely as possible. Maybe we can make something of it. From the looks of things once Hugh finally had a chance to talk to Sally-May he saw that not only was he losing his girl she was about to put her immortal soul in danger."

Nate thought of the interview he'd conducted with John Hugh the night before and frowned; John Hugh, Sally-May and the cult. He didn't want to share this part of the equation out loud but for some reason made him think of the FBI agent and his writer companion. He would get a complete statement from the Nurse then ask the agent and his writer friend in for a chat. Maybe then they'd share.

"The Power and The Blood, I'm a church going man when I get the chance but I have to admit some of these groups bug the hell out of me. It's too damn easy for things to get out of hand. Why the hell did the girl want to talk to us?"

Bill shoved his big hands into his pockets and went through the rest of the story thinking out loud. The sight made Nate smile faintly. This man was tall and broad, a former college football star. A lot of criminals in this area had made the mistake of looking at this man's size and judging him slow and stupid. Most of those who did so ended up behind bars for a long time.

He said, "From what I know of that group the men are pretty used to being obeyed by their woman. I'm thinking our boy saw what's going on and snapped. He picked up the only weapon around, the pillow on the next bed, and took her out. He's a strong looking type and she looked like she'd blow away in a bad wind. Not premeditated murder for sure but its murder. As for wanting to talk to us, maybe she saw some abuse or experienced it herself and wanted to press charges. I don't know. You're right what we need to do is get the nurse in and go over exactly what the kid said and maybe we can figure it out."

"In the mean time I have an idea," said Nate.

He picked up the phone and flipped his phone book to a number. He pressed the numbers and sat listening to the ring. Glancing up at Bill he saw his deputy was confused.

"The fingerprint evidence isn't enough to get him for murder but if we ask them to the hospital will press trespassing charges. That will put him under lock and key and in one place till the DNA results return. I'm passing the word to Jim Young. We could use his help."

Bill made a sour face at this news.

"What do we need some rent-a-cop's help for?" he asked.

Nate sighed deeply and tried to explain without losing his patience.

"His people know this guy on sight. They can double the space we can look. It's no time to get parochial Bill you know better. Anyway Jim's no rent-a-cop he was on the regular force up in Jersey."

"Yeah you're right," the deputy said reluctantly.

Bill turned and started for the office door.

"I'm still gonna get him before they do."

Nate smiled at this example of professional rivalry; far preferable to the derogatory attitude it replaced, and turned full his attention to the phone just as Jim Young answered.

*****

The day progressed in a foggy dream. John worked, he spoke to people, he walked the streets all with the vision of Sally-May's lifeless face. He didn't wonder why wherever he went there was a hovering brother. He was morning his dead love. It seemed natural for them to be there.

Three that afternoon found him standing in the place where he generally set up his podium to preach. In his memory he heard his own voice calling out the truth. He heard other voices questioning him. They always had questions. Only God had the true answers but he had tried to answer in Gods place and many times even the most adamant of his opponents had come to respect his views. An unexpected voice broke into his thoughts.

"Brother you are wasting time. There's the service tonight."

John turned to find Martin standing watching.

"I find my mind wanders on me today," John said. "Still it's only three. There's time."

Martin smiled slightly.

"Not if you are to meet privately with the master before tonight's service," he said.

John stared at Martin trying to read a reason why this announcement had come about in his friend's face and failing. It was strange, almost unprecedented. It was also a little frightening. Then common sense stepped in and he knew there was nothing to be worried over.

"Does he want to ask me about Sally-May?" he asked.

"I have no idea. It's possible. I know he knows what's happened. I'm just doing my duty and following his word," Martin said.

John nodded slightly, "Oh I see."

"We'd better go or we'll both be censured."

Martin led the way to the nearest street. Stunned, past all questioning John simply followed. The Master knew the best way to handle all problems. He would know what to do and that would be the last word on the subject.

*****

"Blessed one come out."

It was time to travel again. David St. John walked out of his small prison eyes on the ground. He was tired, much too tired to fight. The pain would happen, he would be free for a few short moments then the pain would return and he would be here again. Or the machine would malfunction somehow and he would be dead.

The closer he and his escort got to the building where the machine waited the more he noticed the change. Feeling increasingly curious in spite of his resignation David looked around at the crowd. Something was different. There was an extra excitement in the air David did not understand.

The Master was there in position intoning his usual religiously inspired gibberish. The machine was there with its dish pointed toward the sky. The crowd was silent and seemed electrified.

When they arrived at the area where the experiment took place David knew why. Standing beside the master was a naked man. He was not chained. After a long disbelieving look David discovered he recognized the man. This was one of their own people. The shock jolted David out of his listless malaise.

Softly he gasped, "What the hell is going on here?"

He hadn't expected an answer but one of his guards surprised him.

"One of our brothers has asked for permission to take part in the experiment," he explained quietly.

David felt a hysterical laugh well up from his chest. It was impossible, completely impossible.

"You've...you've got to be kidding! Someone's actually ASKED TO DO THIS?" he asked.

The guard's face stayed reverently serious, his eyes held a look of mild reproach.

Sternly he said, "You are being given a privilege. If you continue in this tone you will be returned to your cell."

David bit his lip and swallowed the laugh that wanted to escape. He looked from his guard to the machine. The laugh faded completely.

If they at last admitted that all this thing did was send someone somewhere instantly and painfully then they'd kill him. If they still thought it would get them to heaven while still living then they'd keep zapping him around the map and kill him anyway. Watching this thing from the outside would therefor change nothing for him but from somewhere he felt strength enough to be curious. He really did want to see this event from the outside.

The man stepped into the machine accompanied by two others who attached him to the cross on the inside the huge metal egg. He was calm, his lips moving in a silent prayer. David thought of the times he had been attached in exactly the same way fighting his captors or even yelling and pleading for death. The memory of indignity's past sent a rush of anger and that anger gave him the strength to speak.

"I'll say what I want when I want. There's nothing you can do to me you haven't already done, short of killing me. You're going to do that eventually anyway so frankly Mr. big shot I don't give a damn," he said.

The lid to the gigantic metal egg began to lower. Seeing his view of the world disappear the man inside lost his nerve.

"No. Master I am not worthy," he cried. "Stop! NO!"

David found to his surprise that he had the strength to feel a hint of pity for the hapless volunteer. They'd clearly done a good bit of work on this man to get him to do what he was doing. It almost got him the whole way, almost.

The power was turned on and the entire egg glowed with a strange green aura. The dish began to vibrate and a bright beam shot skyward. The master stepped in front of the crowd then turned and waved toward the machine. David smothered a smile. The man looked like a magician in front of a particularly large and complex trick.

"Open the device," he intoned.

The lid to the egg opened to show the crowd that the man had indeed traveled. The crowd was completely silent. It was a reverence David felt compelled to break. It was an act he immediately knew he'd regret.

"You realize of course he's probably in the middle of Times Square stark naked."

A back-hand blow from the guard that had spoken to him sent David sprawling. Climbing to his feet only half regretting his flippancy he heard the master intone.

"Return our brother so we may know if we have succeeded."

The lid to the egg closed and the man at the control consul began to work. David watched him work listening to the hum of the huge generators that powered the machine and knew something was wrong. The sound from the motors generating the electricity rose in intensity but not far enough. Soft and hesitant, the words slipped out of his mouth before he even knew why he was saying them.

"Something's wrong."

The green aura covered the closed egg. This time it was faint, patchy. David stepped away from his guards toward the controller. They let him go their eyes focused on the big metal egg. There wasn't really any place he could go where they couldn't grab him quickly anyway. If anyone not connected to the creation of this insanity could be said to be an expert in this he was that person.

He knew how it sounded when this thing worked right. He knew how it felt. Something was wrong. Something was seriously wrong and he seemed to be the only one who'd figured it out.

"Your powers not up high enough," he called out. "You at the controls can't you hear it? The generators, they're not making the right sound."

Without thinking David ran forward through the stunned crowd. He gripping the consul and looking down at the working technician. They didn't seem worried. They didn't seem bothered at all.

"This is your own man damn-it! Boost your power or you'll have his atoms scattered all over the eastern seaboard," David yelled.

The sound of the power died. The technician looked up his eyes meeting David's with a fanatical confidence. It was a confidence David found nearly horrific. They knew what they were doing.

"It's done," he said.

The two words confirmed what David already knew.

"You bastard," he gasped. "You did this on purpose didn't you? One of your own! Why?"

The technician pressed a button and the egg opened. The crowd watching gasped and several women screamed. The inside of the egg was a dripping nightmare of deep dark red.

CHAPTER 21

The phone rang Saturday morning jarring Claire out of a deep sleep. Fighting a foggy mind, which would have much preferred to ignore the interruption, she rolled over in bed agreed the receiver then flopped back.

"Hello."

The woman's voice on the line was smooth and sounded frighteningly well organized. Claire immediately wanted to invent a character just like her and have some villain drop her down a well.

"Good morning Miss Anderson I'm Joan Smith executive assistant to Dean Miller. We were wondering Miss Anderson since you are in town anyway if we could hold our social gathering this afternoon instead of Sunday evening. Say, oneish?"

Claire forced her eyes open and looked at the bedside clock. It was a technically civilized nine o'clock. As she had spent much of the night before talking with Kevin St. John the hour did not feel civilized at all.

"Ok sure, where do you want me?" she said hoping simple obedience would substitute for civility.

"The college owns a fine historical home which we use for receptions and other affairs," she said. "I'm told you have met Jim Young our head of security. I've prevailed upon him to escort you."

Claire cringed slightly as she heard the woman's tone of voice as she mentioned the thoughtful knowledgeable professional. It made her new friend sound like a security guard sitting at a desk with a radio, small television and a paperback novel. She wanted to say something but opted for a kind of backwards honesty.

"Head of security," she said, pretending to sound confused. "I thought he was a cop."

"Oh no we have no need for actual policing Miss Anderson. Mr. Young's mandate is simply to ensure our students are protected from any outside element that might be considered undesirable"

Smiling at what was clearly a public relations statement Claire slipped over to the phone's side of the bed and sat up. The night before besides talking, largely about the missing David, she and Kevin had worked their way through a large bottle of red wine. She didn't have a hangover as such, but simply listening to this terribly proper woman was beginning to make her feel a bit nauseated.

"Okay whatever you say. After all I'm just a visitor here. Why the change in schedule from Sunday? It's not just because I'm in town is it? Part of the reason I took this tour on is to give me an excuse to do some traveling. I've spent several years turning out one book after the other. At the same time I was also working a full time day job. I needed a break."

The voice at the other end gave a quiet cough and Clare prepared herself to listen to what she guessed would be yet another public relations statement. She was not disappointed however this one was a bit more forthright.

"Miss Anderson several of our staff are Christians. They object to attending a work related activity, however casual it might be, on the lords day. The Sunday reception was prevailed upon us by the publisher. As you are here anyway we felt it might be possible to change things a bit. You understand I'm sure."

Increasingly tired of this pompous female Claire saw a chance to end the conversation. She ran for it like a miner running for the light at the end of a tunnel about to collapse.

"No problem I understand completely. Oh hey I hear room service must be my breakfast. I'll see you at one."

An half hour later she had showered and dressed and ordered breakfast for real. While waiting for the food she debated how to spend the time till Jim Young would pick her up. Thinking through the problem of filling time found her sitting and turning on her laptop. She fired the machine up and then jumped onto the internet.

The US navy was sure to have a web site if only for reasons of recruitment. An e-mail to the FBI had brought Kevin. Maybe an e-mail to this site, once she found it, would bring someone who would have the authority to do something about people who had the power to zap a person around the map.

She had no doubt at all that a lot could be done under the guise of national security.

Claire found a site that looked promising without too much trouble. Breakfast arrived and nourishment was imbibed while jumping from page to page on the site she located e-mail addresses for four high ranking officers. They were hardly the age's to have been involved in anything connected to World War Two. However their own superiors could very well have served under men of that time period. As military service tended to be a family tradition they might have even had family involved in the event. No matter what the reason it was distantly possible that someone who read what she was about to send would know she was not sending them a fairy story.

After a little careful composing she sent them each the identical e-mail. It was a much different one than what she sent the FBI yet it held the same hard facts. It described several documented appearances of a naked man as discovered by Kevin's partner. It also mentioned the disappearance of an FBI agent before these strange events began. It was very particular about mentioning the Power and The Blood and the general location of their compound.

It did not mention any event that could possibly be connected to her presence. While she did not mind being known by the worried Kevin she had no desire at all to be of interest to the military. Being of personal interest to the military, particularly in a day and age when they could very nearly do anything they wanted legally, was something she defiantly did not want.

Claire turned off her computer and pondered the probable fate of the work she had just done. A series of lowly clerks each working for their respective officer were likely in charge of answering these missives. It's possible it would be read and deleted as a fairy story sent by some crank. However it was just as possible they might look into the matter and that possibility might mean the difference between life and death for David St. John.

The silence of her room was broken, by the ringing of her cell phone. Crossing the room she pulled it out of her purse and answered.

"Claire this is Jim where are you?" he asked.

"I'm in my room at the hotel I've been doing some work," she said.

"Okay don't want to interrupt the creation of another masterpiece so I'll just take a second. I'm told you know about the change in plans. Can I pick you up at about twelve?"

"How about coming early and having a quick lunch?" she asked. "My treat."

"Great idea," he said. "See you at eleven thirty."

*****

Claire and Jim met in the lobby. As they were walking toward the restaurant Kevin entered the lobby from the street. Claire smiled as she saw him. The worried brother of the night before had been transformed in the space of a morning into sharp alert professional.

"Kevin, come and join us for lunch. My treat."

"I'd like that," he said. "We also have something to talk about."

They sat and gave their orders before Kevin continued.

"I've been with the sheriff all morning. He's a good man, very professional. He may not have a lot of experience with this brand of murder but he's well read and has a good idea of how to proceed. One problem though, no one can find John Hugh. He left his apartment yesterday and didn't come home."

"That is a problem," Claire said.

"He must have done it," said Jim. "Nate called my office first thing this morning. My men have been looking for him too. We know he went to his classes yesterday and spent a little time at a job site where he's been working. His cult friends say he was at a prayer meeting out at their retreat last night. No one has seen him since."

"Which is a bit strange," added Kevin. "When people run like this they don't usually go to a prayer meeting first. Even if they do the other worshipers don't admit to their presence."

"He's got to still be at the compound," said Jim.

Kevin shrugged and Claire wondered at the miracle of action. Spending the morning at the Sheriff's side had made this man feel like he was doing something to find his brother. Even though little practical was accomplished that very thing had been enough to completely transform the man who had drank with her the night before.

"He could be but I don't know," Kevin said. "I watched the sheriff question his roommates. They seemed afraid, no, not afraid, terrified. If they knew what he'd done they might protect and hide him but the kind of fear that I saw in these men would be completely out of character. Something's happened."

The waiter brought the food and they began to eat. The hotel had an extensive list of interesting sounding salads that Claire had decided to work her way through. The men had opted for thickly packed sandwiches.

"I'm curious about this retreat of theirs. Do the police have something like an overhead shot of this compound?" Claire asked.

"Way ahead of you. Apparently there's just a general property plan on file in the local planning office. They are very particular about their privacy. On the strength that it might be a spot where a murderer was hiding out I was able to get my people to do a fly over and take pictures. They'll do it this afternoon. We should have some pretty good aerial pictures by tomorrow at the latest."

Claire sighed and attacked the salad she had ordered. Chewing thoughtfully she remembered the voice of the woman on the phone and wondered what the afternoon would bring. If the assistant to the dean was that formidable what on earth was the dean like? The prospect of hanging around and waiting for the pictures with Kevin sounded much more attractive.

She sighed and said, "In the mean time I have to go make nice with total strangers. Total strangers I might add who'll ask me why I don't write literature instead of commercial fiction. Killing pompous English professors is illegal right?"

Jim let loose a broad laugh at this question. Kevin pretended to ponder it seriously.

"I think if you get the right lawyer you could make a case for justifiable homicide."

*****

Contrary to the other two schools this particular affair was strictly a tea, coffee and lemonade social. It was held in a beautiful old mansion, which had been built easily three generations before the civil war.

The upper two floors of this building were used as offices and archival rooms. The ground floor was a series of large rooms' ideal for formal or informal meetings. She had once attended a wedding in a house that was barely half its age and not nearly as grand.

Claire spent the first part of the afternoon in the company of the dean of the school listening to a history of the small college. For the rest of the time she mingled and had conversations that mirrored the other receptions in many ways. However like the young man at the previous school who asked his religiously oriented questions many of the teachers were oddly disturbed by some of the more fantastic aspects of her work.

"Miss Anderson don't you think even in fantasy some images should be avoided? Your book is well written but you have your hero fighting several creatures in this work that seem almost demonic. Is that quite proper?"

Claire studied the woman from her small hat sitting on her carefully styled and heavily sprayed hair to her expensive suit to her matching purse and pumps. She took a moment, breathing deeply and pretending to consider the matter. In reality she was struggling to avoid letting go with the first words which came to her mind. This was no time to be telling anyone they were in need of either a mental enema.

Prepared with a slightly more civilized answer Claire said, "The devil doesn't need me to do his dirty work. There's a world full of repressive governments, environmental rapists, and other such bundles of joy who do his work quite nicely. I'm a storyteller. My work is far less dangerous than over reacting narrow minds that forget the meaning of the word fiction. I assume you are a Christen?"

The woman pouted in a small ladylike way and nodded, clearly confused with the direction Claire was going.

"I am," she said.

"You consider the bible to be literal truth. Am I right?"

The woman stiffened slightly and her chin jutted out noticeably.

"I believe so yes," she said.

Ready for this Claire said, "Okay then answer me this one. If the bible is the word of god and as such deserves reverence certainly the work of an ordinary writer, any ordinary writer, deserves less. The work might be pertinent socially or it may be simple recreation but it's not reality. It's like what Freud said. 'Sometimes a cigar is just a smoke.'"

The woman's mouth fell open and for a long moment she could make nothing but a softly confused gasp.

"Well really!" she said finally.

Claire glanced around and knew she had the attention of the entire room. They might not agree with what she was saying and it was clear many did not but they would talk about this conversation for some time to come. There was no backing out now.

"Yes really. If you want to treat the bible as literal truth that's your privilege. I don't agree with you but I do understand your view and of course agree that you have a right to hold said view. It's when that view leads you to attack things like fantasy and speculative fiction that you drive people like me crazy."

"And why might that be Miss Anderson?" asked the woman.

The icy cold air in the woman's voice produced a sub-arctic silence in the room. The gloves were off now. Claire put her lemonade glass on a nearby table at the same time judging the best rout out of the room and out of the building. Jim Young's questing face came into view. She nodded in the direction of the nearest exit and he seemed to understand. Claire turned to the still waiting professor.

"Madam, from my point of view you belittle the truth you claim to revere by granting everything in print the same power. Just because the words printed in my book are defiantly fiction doesn't mean the words in your book aren't from God. That's what faith is for."

Claire turned and without waiting for an answer left, a quietly smiling Jim Young followed in her wake.

CHAPTER 22

When Jim and Claire got back from the reception Kevin was pacing the lobby. He stopped pacing and greeted them. His voice was a little too loud and his smile a little too broad. To Claire it showed his nervous energy like a floodlight in a darkened theater.

"Hello there. How was your social?" he asked.

"Social nothing it was intellectual war," said Jim energetically. "She jousted with one of the best in the college and in my opinion won."

Kevin's brows raised in surprise. For a moment his nervous energy took a back seat to curiosity.

"This I have to hear about. What happened?" he asked.

"It seems I had delicately chosen words with the head of the English lit department who also has a degree in biblical studies," Claire explained. "Jim thinks I won. She thinks she won. I think it was a draw."

Kevin gave a long loud laugh.

He said, "I bet you won too. You have to tell me all the gory details."

There was no doubt the request was genuine but Claire could see a double reason for the request. Knowing the facts were best left unsaid she was ready to oblige.

"I'll tell you at supper, that is if you're still hanging around when I come down. I need to take off my tea with the dean wear and get into something more comfortable. I also need a stiff drink. University professors are surpassingly hard to handle on lemonade alone. How the kids do it I have no idea."

The slight image of sadness filtered back into the FBI agent's eyes. The amusement he had with her experience was still there but his eyes showed the tension of waiting.

"Can't help you there. If I remember my school years I majored in caffeine," Kevin said. "You go ahead and change I'll be around. I'm waiting on those pictures. They said they'd try and get me the shots tonight instead of first thing tomorrow."

Seeing Claire well settled Jim said, "You kids have a good dinner. Now that I've delivered the conquering hero I've got to get home. My wife may be off traveling but she left me a to-do list a mile long. I wont mind being rescued though. If anything happens you have my cell number give me a call."

The three friends parted company. When Claire came back down to the lobby after changing clothes Kevin was sitting in the hotel's small lounge staring out the window at the deepening twilight. He was completely serious now, his lips a thin line. What looked like scotch and ice sat on a small table in front of him.

Claire slipped into a comfortable chair on the other side of the table and waited for him to speak

"I'm trying to be realistic but every nerve in my body says my brother is still alive and up there in those hills somewhere," he said softly.

Claire gave him a thin smile. The smile that returned hers was like a fleeting shadow. The energetic cheerfulness that had met her in the lobby had faded like picture kept too long in the sun.

"Why did you come here without your partner?" Claire asked. "You said last night he knows all about it."

Kevin shook his head slightly but firmly and said;

"He does. He wanted to come. I wouldn't let him. I guess my mind was working overtime. I knew if the e-mail you sent was even half right I might have to brake more than a few rules. If it gets my brother back alive I don't mind losing my job or even going to jail but I won't pull another man into that kind of situation."

Kevin sipped his drink and sat watching the ice cubes dance in the amber liquid. Feeling the worry radiating from the man in front of her Claire searched for something to say. His eyes went from the drink in his hands to the street in front of the hotel.

"So, they'll send you the pictures as soon as they have them," she said.

As an attempt at a conversation it felt lame but functional. It gave him a chance to say something and this man defiantly needed to talk.

He said, "They'll be sending a set to me and one to the sheriff. I told them I'd be waiting here or in my room. The desk has instructions to find me and wake me up if necessary."

Feeling slightly maternal Claire nodded toward the entrance to the restaurant. The place was beginning to fill up. If they were going to get a table on this weekend evening they probably should move.

She said, "Well, if you're going to be ready to dash off into the night and be heroic you need to eat. Let's go. I'll tell you all about my afternoon of lemonade and literature chat."

He looked around and it was obvious he reluctantly agreed that food was necessary. The small menu on each of the tables caught his eyes.

"We can eat in here can't we?" he asked. "Why move?"

Claire smiled again knowing what he was really saying. The restaurant on the other side of the lobby had no clear view of the street. In his mind the pictures would be there any minute and he wanted to have them the second they arrived. Claire picked up the small menu that sat in a stand on the table between them and looked at the food on offer.

"Why move indeed," she said. "Besides I did say I wanted a drink didn't I. Tavern food it is."

*****

Claire stayed with Kevin in the bar till ten then suggested that they each needed a decent night's sleep. Reluctantly he agreed and they both went to their separate rooms and bed.

Claire woke to the sound of the room next door being vacuumed. Fumbling for the phone she ordered food and then reluctantly crawled from the bed's warmth and dressed. She had finished her food and the last of her pot of tea that went with the food when there was a knock on her door. A look through the door's peephole showed Jim Young standing on the other side. She opened the door wide so he could enter. He stood in the hall radiating a tense energy that put Claire's nerves on edge.

"Hi, finish all your to-do's?" she asked uncertainly. "Jim is there something wrong? You look prickly."

Claire frowned. Something about the way the man in front of her moved or just stood in her room surveying its contents said this wasn't Jim Young her new friend. It was Jim Young, cop.

"I did some," he said. "And yes something might be wrong. I got home from church this morning to find a message from the sheriff on my machine. He's trying to get in touch with Kevin and thought he might be with me. Is he here?"

Claire shook her head firmly and said; "I'm fond of him Jim but not that fond. Besides he's engaged. I'm not the sort to fish in another woman's pond. Is this about the shots of the compound?"

The man in front of her looked curiously disappointed and even more worried.

"Sorry I didn't mean anything by that I thought maybe you were having breakfast or something," Jim stopped closed his eyes took a deep breath and let it go. "Okay before I dig myself in any deeper lets forget about that and just move on."

Smothering a laugh Claire said, "Agreed."

Jim said, "They told me down stairs that the aerial shots were delivered here around midnight. I haven't seen them but after the Sheriff got a good look at his set when he came in this morning he called me and gave me the low down. He wants me to glue my behind to Kevin, if he's still around. I better see if he's in his room."

He started away from her door walking down the hall without looking back. Moving briskly Jim's feet made soft but decisive thumps on the thickly carpeted hall.

"Hang on wait for me," Claire called.

She quickly grabbed her bag and room key and followed. They reached Kevin's room together and Jim pulled out a hotel key.

"How'd you get that," Claire asked.

Seeing the confusion in Claire's face he said,

"Management gave me the passkey. One of the advantages in working in a small town is you get to know everyone and everyone knows what your about. Technically speaking this is even legal I'm acting on the request of the sheriff who wants me to make sure Kevin is okay. I just want to make sure he's here."

"Where would he be if not in his room?" Claire asked. "I mean I assume you checked downstairs."

With the door opened she and Jim entered a vacant hotel room identical to Claire's except the window looked out in the opposite direction. A table next to the window was covered in large photographs. Jim went straight to the table and began sifting through the pile. He stopped at one looked at it for a long minute and dropped it to the table on the top of the pile.

Softly he said, "Damn. There it is. The reason why he's not here and probably the motivation for doing something monumentally stupid."

Claire looked at it and her mouth fell open in shock.

The compound seemed to consist of a series of different sized buildings. All one story. In the center of a large clearing was a small shed. In front of this shed were two posts and standing with his arms spread out and one wrist chained to each post was a naked man.

"It's hard to see from this angle but even I say that could be David," she said. "And I only saw him a couple of times under unusual circumstances. What's the sheriff doing about this?"

"There's a chance they're making John Hugh do some strange kind of penance or something. He'd certainly confess to the leader if to no one else so that makes sense. It's more likely your right and this is David St. John. The Sheriff is consulting with the feds. If they can prove to a judge that this is the missing David St. John or even our murder suspect then this is will get us our search warrant."

Claire felt her heart beat in her temples. The small strange situation she stumbled into while standing on her verandah in the middle of the night was about to grow very big very quickly.

"Right. That's just perfect," she muttered. "Warrant or no warrant, they have a great record for dealing with isolated religious strong holds don't they?"

Jim face went hard.

"I have to go," he said simply.

He dropped the picture onto the table and headed back out into the hall. Claire followed hovering uncertainly as he closed the hotel room door. She tried to look him in the eyes. He wouldn't let her.

"Jim?" she said hesitantly. "Wait a second. Where are you going?"

Jim looked around at the empty hall. They were alone. He opened his mouth then closed it as if searching for just the right words.

"Claire, Kevin knows the FBI's record in situations like this. Hell who doesn't?" he said finally. You want to guess where he's going? You want to guess where he is right now?"

Jim started for the stairwell and began walking down the two floors to the lobby. Claire followed in his wake wishing her imagination wasn't working overtime. Her imagination was her only real asset yet at times of great stress it tended to feed her pictures that were far from reassuring.

In her mind's eye she could see the skilled driven FBI agent taking his car as far as the roads would go then walking carefully through the wood. She could see him spending the day watching the compound. She could then see him breaking into the compound to get his imprisoned brother back. In her mind's eye she saw him getting caught. They reached the bottom of the stair well before she spoke.

"Jim this isn't a book it's for real," she said. "You can't mean he's gone up there alone. Surely that goes against all of his training? I mean surely the cop shows get some of this stuff right, you just don't do this sort of thing without backup."

Jim turned to face her, his hand on the door that would let him into the lobby. As he spoke she found herself wondering if it was more than worry for his kids that had brought him away from New Jersey. Looking into his eyes she knew she was right. This man had made his own share of questionable choices and he knew they were almost always made for what sounded like the right reason.

He said, "Claire, men do stupid heroic stuff all the time. They do it for real not just in books. Now if you'll excuse me I have to see if I can stop a man from being stupid heroic and dead."

He pushed through the door and entered the lobby. After tossing the clerk at the desk the passkey he strode through the lobby and out into the street. Following an impulse she didn't understand Claire stayed at his side.

"I'm coming too," she said.

"You are like hell," he barked. "This is big boy's play-time Claire. You aren't equipped for this!"

Claire knew he was right. Still she couldn't make her feet stop moving. She was here at the start of this strange nightmare and she wanted to see it through.

"I can stay with the car," she said, grasping at an idea. "You can't just leave it they're sure to try and do something to it. I can sit there and write poetry and tell anyone that asks that this is what I do on Sundays. I'm a writer who the hell knows what writers do on their days off?"

They stopped by Jim's car, an unmarked blue jeep. Jim leaned on the roof clearly struggling with what she had said yet Claire could see she had struck a chord. He clearly didn't like it but there was logic here he could not deny.

"Okay so that makes at least a little sense," he said. "There's one problem. A lot of these people are students. You probably even met a couple at the social yesterday. Why are you driving my car?"

It took Claire's plot generating mind a mere half- second to explain that one.

She said, "Simple. I drive an ordinary hatch back and it's not in the best of shape. I wanted a four-wheel drive to handle the hills and borrowed yours. After all it's your day off and you're home mowing the lawn."

He rolled his eyes and ran his right hand through his short dark hair. His left still stayed on the Jeeps hard top roof as if relishing the solid security it represented.

174

"You're right. It makes sense. You could even go for help if I don't come back on time," he said reluctantly. "And I mean that. You don't follow. You run away."

"Hey I live for heroically running away," she said. "So, lets go."

Claire waited for him to open the car door. Instead he stood as if thinking. Claire was immediately suspicious.

He said, "I have to stop at the sheriff's office to get a map and find out from him where the best place to watch the compound might be, then we can go."

He made as if to open the passenger door then stopped.

"Wait a second you'll need to go back and get a notepad or something wont you?" he asked.

Ready for him Claire smiled and pulled her palm pilot out of her purse. The casually delivered line had been a transparent ruse to get her to leave him alone for a moment so he could drive away.

"We modern poets scoff at note pads. It even has a couple of novels downloaded into it in case I get bored," she said.

He stared at her momentarily at a loss for words.

"Your unshakable you know that?" he said.

She said, "Of course I am. I'm a published writer Jim. No matter how good you are just getting published takes the persistence of a charging rhino."

He opened the jeep's passenger door and stood waiting for her to enter.

"All right I give up," he said. "Get in."

*****

Three of the e-mails send by Claire, were read by the serious minded clerks who opened them. Understandably they were considered typical internet fairy stories and deleted. The fourth was read and enjoyed as the well-written typical internet fairy story it clearly was then printed up and delivered with the morning mail. It was sent as a joke. His boss had a position that tended to involve a lot of stress and liked a good laugh. The clerk liked to oblige when he could.

The officer read the note and as his clerk knew he would laughed out loud. Later that morning he met a friend in a corridor he pulled out the note and passed it on. Both men had a good laugh over the blatant tabloid fiction. A third man simply passing them in the hall overheard their conversation and asked for the two sheets of paper.

He stood at five foot ten inches tall with a compact build. His hair was short and gray, his uniform immaculate. His first name was Don; his true family name was lost in a maze of security clearances and red tape. Whenever he needed one he tended to use the name Smith.

Don read the e-mail. The text hit him with a wave of shocked disbelief yet that feeling did not come close to touching his face. He looked up and fixed the two other officers with a sharp eye that stopped their good humor cold. He knew who they were but what was more important, they knew what he was. His instructions to them were simple and to the point.

"You didn't get this. You didn't read it. You didn't talk about it. It never happened," he said. "You better tell anyone who's come anywhere near this the same thing. I trust I'm being understood gentlemen?"

Don turned from their questioning eyes without waiting for an answer and began walking. The two men he left stood watching him go mouths opened with unasked questions. They knew better to ask and he had no obligation to answer.

By the time Don passed a barrier protected by armed guards and electronic screening he had totally forgotten the officer's confused disbelieving looks. The guards at the barrier jumped to attention letting him pass without challenge. The electronic screening equipment beeped once and was silent. He continued along a long stark hallway and entered a huge room full of filing cabinets.

Some secrets could be trusted to computers. Others needed the security of ink on paper in a room that didn't exist. Under conditions like this one need only a shredder to grant that secret total oblivion.

Don Smith traveled in circles that knew for a fact it was better far better for some secrets to vanish without a trace than for them to be known by the wrong person. In the middle of this room a clerk sat typing on a computer. Don had never asked his name and no name not even a false one had ever been offered.

"He in?" Don asked.

"Yes sir."

Don passed through the room to an unmarked door. He walked through the door without knocking and entered a small windowless office. The man working at the desk was just over seventy years old. He looked no more than sixty. He had a bland unremarkable face with eyes that betrayed the detailed knowledge of every secret ever kept in the room leading to his. Don knew he had a name and he even knew what that name was in spite of this he tended to simply call him Mother.

"Morning mother."

The man looked up his brows arching in mild surprise. The surprise changed very quickly to concern.

"So nice when the children come for a surprise visit," Mother said faintly. "You haven't looked like that in a while Don what's wrong?"

The question had a two-word answer.

"Read this."

Mother did as he was asked looking up only when he was finished. His lined face held a look that was half way between astonishment and anger.

He said, "My god that lunatic did it. Using university students and working with less than a quarter of the budget he did what dozens of our people couldn't. That's why we left him alone all this time. I didn't think it was possible. No one did."

Don stood in front of the desk his face a picture that was half rueful acceptance half annoyance.

He said, "Never underestimate the power of a sick old man or the people he gathers around him. Maybe our people should have been trying to get to heaven instead. It seems to have worked for the group."

Mother put both pages on his desk side by side. He laid a hand on each page as if willing the answer to the situation to come from the paper itself.

"Indeed. Faith seems to have moved a mountain. Or perhaps I should say a man. We have clearly been somewhat arrogant in our disregard," he said faintly.

"We have to pull his plug," said Don.

"Most assuredly so," Mother said.

Throwing off the sudden thoughtful mood the man at the desk nodded in agreement. This was a situation that was unexpected but not completely. Theirs was a business that specialized in being prepared for everything, even the impossible.

"Do it. Get the equipment. Get the man they've been experimenting on. He can walk when we're finished looking him over but we need to know what that machinery has done to him. He'll probably want to know himself so he should be a willing patient. If he really is an FBI agent then security issues should be a formality."

"I have full permission?" Don asked.

The man Don called Mother looked up from behind the desk his face bland and emotionless. They both knew what full permission meant. It was a phrase that held in it the full spectrum of possibilities from the routinely expedient to the deadly.

"Act quietly and with care but shut this thing down."

CHAPTER 23

Kevin had spent some of his time waiting for the overhead photographs, studying the maps he had of the area intently. Making use of this knowledge he found a side road that ran parallel to cult land. He parked his car at what he hoped was a respectable distance then carefully made his way through the pre-dawn wood to a sheltered vantage point.

Crouching in the damp undergrowth he pulled a camera with a telephoto lens out of the backpack of equipment he had brought. Adjusting the setting he trained it on the dimly lit compound. His hands trembled as he tapped the shutter button. It took every inch of his strength to hold in the scream that threatened to break the silence of the swiftly ending night.

A man was half standing half hanging, his arms chained to two out-stretched posts. It was just as it had been in the aerial photo. Only from here there was no question it was David.

Dawn was touching the sky. Four strong men came out of one of the buildings. They freed David, half carrying him to the small isolated shed in the middle of the compound. Pressing the shutter button again and again Kevin recorded all of this so it could be used in evidence.

Training his telephoto lens at the shed door he could easily see the thing was locked by padlock. It was strong but not strong enough to defeat the metal cutters he'd brought with him.

"It's just a matter of time now David," he thought. "You hang on."

Now that it was light enough to see his surroundings in detail Kevin trained his camera on the compound itself. There seemed to be no security at all till Kevin noticed small cameras. The sight put a lump in his throat.

"Closed circuit security," he muttered. "Someone isn't trusting just god. This is going to be harder than I thought."

The light grew and the day began. People from outside joined those who seemed to live on site and morning prayers were held in the open space in the center. The group then disbanded some to various buildings many went back the way they came, down the road that led back to town.

The longer he watched the operation of the cult stronghold the colder the feeling in his gut became. There was no way of denying the truth. This was not a one-man operation. Even if that man was as driven and motivated as himself.

Without the cameras it would be simple, cut the wire fence, run to the shed, cut the lock and get David out. The cameras made doing that undetected practically impossible. In this case the only thing to do would be an all-out raid. They had to take the group by surprise before they could do anything to their hostage.

Kevin put the camera back in his backpack and slowly carefully began to make his way back to the car. Suddenly something felt wrong. He stopped and looked around at the wood. A bird flew from one tree to another. Other than that the air was silent.

He neared the road and stepped out onto the gravel. The car was gone. This meant one thing only. He was in serious trouble. He dropped his backpack labeling it as excess baggage and stepped out onto the road facing the direction he came. Either the cameras had spotted him after all or someone from the prayer meeting had spotted his car. It didn't matter which had brought him to this point, they were there and he was alone.

"Aw shit."

*****

David lay on his bed, body aching from the twenty-four hours standing arms outstretched. The penance for misbehaving at the experiment. Floating in an exhaustion fed haze he heard faint sounds outside his small dark pocket that were different.

After weeks of imprisoned sameness something very new and different was happening. Faintly David recognized the sounds of physical battery. A man cried out in anger using a selection of words his captors never used even when furious. David had been around these people more than long enough to know no matter what else this man had done this sacrilege was going to cost him. Moments later the voice called out in wordless pain and David knew he'd guessed right.

Strangely the sounds began to grow louder and softer at the same time, as if the victim were losing energy yet drawing closer. Then the door to the shed was unlocked. David cringed against the sudden flood of bright light as two large men dragged a third into the gloom and dropped him on the floor. The door slammed shut and the outside world faded into distant movement and sound.

"Who are you?" David asked.

"A stupid idiot."

The soft voice that filled the darkness hit David like a body blow. He felt a scream like a grieving wail build in his chest. He stuffed a fist into his mouth closing off the cry. It took everything he had to change the feeling into simple sorrow filled words.

"Oh God Kevin, no," he gasped. "It isn't you. I'm not listening to this."

The answer was quiet. The voice breathy as if its owner had been hit hard more than a few times in the stomach and the act of breathing deeply to speak was a struggle. There was no denying it was Kevin.

"The office knows you're here David. They did a fly over yesterday when you were outside. I was going to break you out myself. I was afraid of what might happen if they did some kind of big maneuver. Then I spotted the security cameras so I just took some pictures. I thought where I was I was out of the sight of the cameras. I was backing off when I found they'd stolen my car. If you don't mind I'd rather not talk about the rest its kind of embarrassing."

David stifled a bitter laugh.

He said, "Kevin you're talking to a man who's spent the last god knows how many weeks naked. What's it been eight weeks? Ten? Longer? I can't remember. I don't think very clearly these days."

David listened to the darkness. It sounded as if Kevin were trying to sit up. The movement stopped and David assumed his brother had given up the prospect of sitting and was simply stretched out on the floor. "Okay fair enough. The short form version is they ran me down like a scared rabbit, beat the crap out of me and chained my hands behind my back," Kevin said.

David smiled at this sparse explanation.

"Bet you got a few licks in though," he said.

Faint memories of brotherly conversations of the past ran through David's head. A lot of them involved one brother trying to outdo the other. Somewhere along the line he had an idea the balance was never quite equal. It was too late for apologies, far too late.

"Hey, I don't spend all my time behind a desk you know," Kevin said. "I think a couple of them might have ended up with broken bones. Would have done a lot more but I lost my gun in about the first two seconds."

David smiled into the darkness. It was too late to apologize for being a show off. It wasn't too late to let his brother have one last win.

He said, "For the record bro you did better than I did. They lured me in here without a hint of a problem then had me naked and flat on the ground with some jerk sitting on my back in three minutes flat and not one of them had a scratch on him."

The satisfaction this simple trading of stories gave David was overshadowed by a bitter truth. They were both here. They were both going to die and the only child their parents would have left would be their younger sister.

Moving slowly and stiffly David rolled over on his small narrow cot and reached out with his manacled hands. He found his brothers shoulder and gave what he hoped was an understanding and supportive squeeze before subsiding back on his bed.

He said, "Kevin the bureau is the best at a lot of things but dealing with groups like this...."

"I know. That's why I came up here alone. Then once I was up here I had to admit to it just wasn't a one-man operation. I was backing away but either they spotted me on the cameras or one of those people who were at that prayer meeting must have spotted my car. Dumb stupid bad luck."

A vivid memory of dripping red gore invaded David's mind. With a huge effort he shook it off but the reality it represented could not be ignored. He licked his dry lips and struggled to keep his voice calm.

"My vote is for the camera's but it doesn't matter. The thing is Kev, any sort of raid is going to take time. We might not be here if they do get it right. These people have a way of killing you and not leaving a body."

"The teleportation machine."

"How do you know about that?"

David was completely taken off guard and it showed in his voice. The soft laugh pained laugh that answered him painted a picture. His younger brother was in rough shape but still able to appreciate getting one up on his big brother.

"Well, since the only thing that doesn't hurt on me is my mouth I guess I might as well tell the whole thing, that is if they give us the time," he said.

"Brother I'm all ears."

*****

Without knowing it Jim Young backed his jeep into the exact spot Kevin St. John had taken mere hours before. He stopped the car and turned to face Claire. His eyes gripped hers and Claire began to regret her refusal to be taken in by his attempt to leave her behind at the hotel.

"Now that we're here I want you to listen to me," he said. "You have to do exactly what I say. Both our lives could depend on it and I'm not kidding here. These people play for real."

"No problem," she said.

They both got out of the car. Claire circled the front and watched as Jim took a lawn chair out of the back of the jeep. He set the chair next to the open door of the driver's side. He then opened the rear passenger door and continued his instructions.

"If you hear me coming fast and yelling toss the chair out of the way get in the car and get it started up. When I jump in the back you get us out of here and drive very fast. Someone jumps in front of the car, drive over them. And one more thing."

Claire found her heart thumping hard in her chest. The reality of what she was involved in had hit her nervous system. Silently she wished she could be almost anywhere else.

"Okay what?" she said.

"I'm not going to be watching them," he explained.

"I'm going to be staying as far away from the compound as possible and looking for Kevin. What we're here to do is grab him and get him out of the way before he does something stupid. I'll give one hour to looking and then start back. You give me two hours no more than two and a half then get the hell out. Remember Claire, running for help is not cowardice. Its doing what you can with the skills you have."

Then he was gone and Claire was alone surrounded by a silence that was comforting and at the same time more than a little unsettling. A bird, clearly used to picnickers providing crumbs flew down and eyed her questioningly. Disappointed it flew off.

Claire pulled her palm pilot out of her purse then tossed the bag back into the car. After some thought she used the tool to write a short poem about self-important feathered friends. It was an action that added a small scrap of reality in an unreal situation.

Time passed and a rabbit moved into her line of sight. Delighted with this Claire simply sat and watched the little animal hop through the tall grass that filed the space between the rutted dirt and gravel road and the trees. When it finally moved leisurely out of sight Claire wrote three short poems about small animals unconcerned with danger and enjoying life.

Time passed and buzzing warm weather bugs made Claire sleepy. She slid the stylus belonging to palm pilot into its holder and switched to reading one of the downloaded books its memories held. The book was a space adventure written by a friend and self-published with an electronic press. It wasn't very good but she had promised to read and report her thoughts. Wondering how you could say, "This thing is crap you'll never get any conventional press to take it." and still preserve their friendship Claire looked up at her surroundings.

She was hoping for another glimpse of the rabbit. The rabbit was gone but something in a pile of leaves next to the road where the animal had been caught her eye. Claire stood slipped her palm pilot into a pocket and walked the twenty feet along the road to where this dark thing sat half buried in dead leaves. It was a gun.

Picking it up by the barrel as she had seen on police shows she examined the weapon. There were no signs of blood. A bird flew out of the trees and distantly Claire could hear running. Without thinking she dropped the gun in her jacket pocket and ran back to the car. Tossing the chair aside she got behind the wheel closed her door and started the car.

Heart thumping hard Claire looked back at the trees. A single shadowy figure was running. Three other figures were chasing and as she watched they caught up with their prey.

Fighting the urge to call out Claire watched as two of the figures held what she now knew was Jim Young. The third then began pounding him in the stomach. He pulled out of their arms and tried to fight back but they had the advantage of numbers and in a painfully short time he was sagging in their arms.

There was no way he was going to be able to break away from this. Claire reached into the back and pulled the door that she now knew he would not be jumping into closed. It was time to fulfill her purpose in coming along on this little excursion. Time to drive like hell and get help.

CHAPTER 24

With Claire almost standing on the gas the Jeep took off in a way that sprayed gravel and caused Claire's stomach to lurch sluggishly. Thankfully no men jumped out onto the road ready to force her to stop, or get run over for their troubles. The only men in sight seemed to be concentrating their attentions on their captive. Faintly aware she was going far too fast to be safe considering the state of the road she was driving on Claire put the spot behind her.

Blinking fear-fueled tears from her eyes Claire had to grip the wheel hard to prevent her hands from shaking. They had three of them now. What was more important they had definite evidence the outside world had stopped ignoring them. Something drastic had to happen very fast or all three of those men would be dead.

The trees lining the narrow road widened and Claire knew she was reaching the larger smoothly graded gravel road that would lead in turn to the paved and busy highway. A car appeared at the intersection. It took Claire a full two seconds to absorb the fact that the car was not moving away. It was blocking the road. A man got out of the car holding a rifle.

A quick look at either side of the intersection made driving around the obstruction even in the Jeep a good way to wreck the car and get caught. The soft shoulder was much to narrow. Beyond the road's soft shoulder was a deep drainage ditch tailor made for getting stuck in, even for a jeep.

Faintly remembering a side road Claire for the first time in her life used a trick taught her by a boyfriend in one of those unsupervised after-midnight moment's parents dread and young people remember forever. Remembering the moves as if the night were a week ago instead of nearly twenty years distant for the first time in her life Claire "pulled a donut". She stepped on the breaks and spun the wheel. As if she were sitting in an adventure ride at a theme park Claire's view of the world turned with stomach spinning speed. Once pointed in the direction she had been coming from Claire all but stood on the gas-peddle and took off back up the road. Behind her, an explosion echoed and a spray of buckshot hit the trunk.

Praying for the four-wheel drive car to be as solid as the commercials claimed Claire found the side road, which was little more than a narrow path. She shot down it and out of the sun's harsh glare entering a tunnel of tree covered green.

Tree branches slapped the car bending and cracking as she forced the vehicle through the narrow space. Saplings fell under her wheels only to jump up looking worse for the experience but still alive. Something brown and furry ran terrified along the path then dashed off into the underbrush. All the while the jeep bounced like a bucking bronco.

Claire had no idea where she was going. She had no idea how to get to where she could find help. She only knew staying in one spot meant capture and probably death. The jeep crossed a small stream. The wheels lost traction in the slippery mud and began to skid. With no room to recover from the skid the jeep crashed head on into a tree.

Stunned but not hurt Claire jumped out from behind the wheel. Leaving her bulky purse behind she began to run. Faint echoes of men's voices drifted through the wood spurring her on. Changing direction again and again she ran faster and over rougher terrain than she had ever done before.

She fell and lay stretched out on the ground her aching throbbing leg muscles telling her a sad truth. She was in reasonable shape for a woman who practiced a sedentary craft but she had never in her life been an athlete. There was no way she could keep this up for much longer.

A long pile of leaves filling an open gash in the ground caught her eye. The faint memory of an action film ran through her mind. Half crawling half diving for the leaves she dug down fast. In less than a minute Claire put her entire body a good three or four inches under the blanket of leaves.

Closing her eyes she struggled to get her deep loud rasping breath back to normal. She had to stay still, breathe quietly. She had to be invisible. She had just about managed the feat and was actually feeling as if she were going to doze off when voices came into hearing range.

At first the voices were faint then two sets of shoes came within ten feet of where she lay. The voice of a young man spoke up in frustration.

"Where the hell did the bitch go?" he asked.

An older voice reprimanded him.

"Blaspheming Aaron."

"Shove it will you?" said the annoyed Aaron. "That woman gets away no one is going anywhere, particularly to heaven."

A man's shoe stepped into the pile of leaves a mere five inches away from Claire's head. It moved at the sound of the older man's voice.

"These things are sent to try us Aaron," the older man said.

"You don't get it do you," Aaron snapped. "They killed John Hugh. The blessed one said they did it deliberately and I think I believe him. They won't tell us why. They won't even admit that's what happened. They sent the Blessed one back and forth a dozen times and more and no problems. One of us goes and he's toast. If anyone else does something wrong they'll end up the same way. That's what censure is going to end up meaning. It's not going to mean you do penance it's going to mean you're dead. I'm scared Mat. This thing is going way wrong, real fast."

There was silence for a moment then the older man Claire now knew as Mat spoke again. There was a tone in his voice that told Claire he had heard every word the younger man had said and probably agreed. At the same time he'd been around to know the wisdom inherent in keeping your mouth shut.

"I think the woman might have double back," Mat said. "She has clearly not come this way. Why would she? It's too close to the compound."

"I want out Mat," said Aaron.

To Claire it seemed as if this was something the younger man had wanted to say out loud for a long time. He had started talking now and compulsively it was hard for him to stop. Considering what he had been talking about earlier it was also a thing with the potential for danger.

Mat said, "Aaron we must do our duty for the moment. In twenty-four hours your time will be your own. Then you must do what your heart tells you."

A thick silence filled the air. Claire could guess what the younger man was thinking. Under the same circumstances she would probably be thinking it herself.

"You won't tell?" he asked.

"That's not my way," Mat said firmly. "Lets go."

The voices and footsteps faded from Claire's hearing. She tried to move and found her mind could grasp nothing but a deep desire to lay still and think of nothing. Her back was pressed against the cool comforting earth. The leaves that covered her gave off the soothing smell of fall days past. Darkness overcame her mind and she slept.

*****

Jim Young sat hunched against the wall of a garage, hands cuffed behind his back. He felt very much like a prisoner of war.

They'd been dragged to this place fighting all the way. It had been useless effort. They had the advantage of numbers. By the time the old man had come to question him the only thing he had the strength to do was keep silent. It wasn't easy but he had experience.

Once in another life he had worked narcotics. A yearlong undercover operation had come down to one large buy and the seller had not trusted he was for real. He'd kept his cover and the sting had captured a good-sized importer of high-grade cocaine.

Once the trial had finished however his boss and his wife had read him out the facts of life. The bad guys knew who he was now so even as a conventional detective in another department he was in danger. He had two kids and wife who needed him. Resumes had been sent and they had moved south.

Clearly dissatisfied with his failure to make his prisoner speak the Master turned to his followers. Dimly behind a curtain of pain Jim heard that the ceremonial tone to the man's voice vanish. He no longer sounded like a preacher on a pulpit or actor on stage as he had when he first walked into the building and faced his prisoner. He was now an executive managing a difficult problem. He also had a painfully accurate idea of what that problem was even without help from his silent prisoner.

"What he does not say speaks volumes. This means he has experience or training; this labels him, police or perhaps ONI. Hold him here. Something must be done. We must call the seniors. It will be done tonight."

"Should he be prepared Master?" asked one of the flunkies.

"No. Our plans are changed. We must sacrifice ceremony at the altar of expediency."

Time passed. It had been late afternoon when he had been taken. Though he could not see outside the air in the garage now had the feel of early evening. Whatever was due to happen would happen soon.

Confirming his guess a door opened. A man stood in the opening.

"We're ready for him."

Jim stiffened as his keepers walked toward him. The two largest each grabbed an arm and they pulled him to his feet. He stumbled slightly and realized he had very little fight left.

Once outside he saw that one large building had been opened up. A machine was half in half out with a thing that looked like a radar dish pointed toward the sky. Standing in front of this was a large group of men.

Two things held the attention of these men. One was the machine and the old man the others had called master. The other was a pair of men. Looking as if he were barely able to stand Kevin St. John's mouth fell open.

"Oh god Jim not you too," he said.

With swollen lips Jim managed a limp crooked smile.

He said, "Bad luck knows no boundaries I guess The sheriff sent me to find you and get you out of the way before you did something stupid. I was a bit late."

The Masters voice rang out silencing any further attempt at conversation.

"My loyal friends," he said addressing the crowd. "Our savior was crucified with two thieves. It is clear to me that the appearance of these two who have tried to steal away the Blessed one is a message. What was done in the past must be done again. We will make this final sacrifice and then retreat to more private accommodations to study what we have learned."

The big egg shaped compartment that was the central part of the machine opened to show a cross. Jim immediately understood the metal crucifies he had seen so many times. One man grabbed David St. John's arm and marched him forward. The man went moving as if in a daze. Jim inched closer to Kevin.

"He looks bad," Jim said.

"They put us in together," Kevin said. "He was talking and basically okay when we were locked up. He's been practically catatonic since they walked us over here. I think he knows what's going to happen."

"He knows or he thinks he does," said Jim.

Jim watched, fascinated in spite of himself as David was attached to the crossbars that hovered in the center of the metal ball. At a wave of the masters hand Jim found himself pulled toward the egg. Moving too fast for him to protest or fight the men picked him up bodily and dumped him into the metal ball so he fit underneath the crossbars where David was bound.

"What the hell is going on?" he gasped not really expecting an answer.

Surprising him David answered.

"They're going to kill us," he said. "They'll use Kevin as a Blessed one now. It'll be hard but at least he'll be alive. When the bureau gets around to raiding the place he'll be here. I made a stupid mistake and got caught. I'm sorry for you too whoever you are but he's my brother. I don't want my brother to die because of my mistake."

His voice was calm, accepting. He was going to die but his brother was going to live. Then something happened outside the mettle ball in which he crouched. Jim couldn't see outside to know what it was but it broke his companion's shell of fatalistic acceptance.

"NO. No you can't! What about the sacrifice? What about getting to heaven? NO! OH GOD NO!"

A badly battered Kevin St. John was forced into the metal egg from the opposite side so that it did not quite land on top of Jim. Kevin looked up at his brother. The pain in his eyes made Jim close his own. He was about to die himself yet the vision of brothers dying together was too much to watch.

Somewhere outside a turbine began to hum.

*****

Claire woke up from her exhaustion driven nap and pushed aside the leaf litter to find it was pitch dark. Dreaming vividly of the small flashlight in her purse she felt her way from tree to tree with only the stars and quarter moon for illumination. A faint glow began to show through the trees. Heart thumping hard in her chest, she, following the light, she, praying it was the highway.

It wasn't the highway. Instead Claire found she had stumbled within ten feet of the chain link fence surrounding the floodlit cult compound. Blind good luck had brought her to what was probably the only part of the fence safe enough to stand close to without immediately being seen. Twenty yards from the fence stood a large one story building. There wasn't a cult member in sight.

"FOR PITTY SAKE DON'T KILL MY BROTHER!"

The heart-rending plea came from the other side of the building Claire faced. She didn't know the voice but it painted a desperate picture that demanded action. Hating the truth Claire knew there was no one left to act.

She pulled the gun she had found out of her pocket then stopped. She didn't know much about guns but one this size held six or seven bullets, nine at most. In the hands of someone who knew what they were doing it might help. In her hands it would do next to nothing. Then she looked at the building. A machine that could successfully teleport a man would have a massive amount of computing hardware, not to mention the power generating equipment to run the machine.

"Okay boys prepare for a computer crash."

If they were using the thing to kill their prisoners and dispose of the bodies then a few well-placed bullets would stop that from happening. They would have to kill their prisoners some other way. All of the other ways her writers mind could think of left evidence. It wouldn't stop them from being killed but it would jail their killers. That would have to be enough.

Remembering that guns, even small handguns, had a kick when fired Claire braced her back against a tree and aimed the weapon at the corrugated metal wall. Praying hard that this would work she held the gun in both hands the same way she had seen on police shows then squeezed the trigger.

CHAPTER 25

Ears ringing with the huge explosive bangs made by the gun in her hands Claire squeezed the trigger until it simply makes small clicking sounds. Only when this relative silence returned did she hear the response to the shots. The response was satisfying and terrifying all at once.

Yells of fear, indignation and pain were coming from the other side of the building. Knowing that no matter how confused they might be momentarily they would soon be after her. Claire turned and ran into the wood.

She got ten feet and ran straight into a black cloth wall. Firm hands gripped her and pulled the gun from her hands. She fought back blindly till a deep and faintly amused voice said;

"Hold it lady; I'm one of the good guys."

The words helped Claire calm down enough to actually look at the man she had run into. The light coming through the trees from the nearby compound showed a man in black battle gear complete with a communication's head set and a compact night vision lens that could be flipped over one eye. He was clearly not a cult member. She didn't think local police had this sort of equipment either.

"Who are you?" Claire gasped.

"Navy, special op's," he said simply. "You know the good guys."

The man turned his attention to a headset he wore and said, "Random signal wrapped up. Move in. I want this place in our hands in five seconds as of now."

The strangely compelling man dropped the empty pistol into a pocket then grabbed her hand and led the way around the compound. Taking a path that ran right by the chain link fence they walked out in the open as casually as if he was taking her on an evening stroll. As they went they saw two large almost silent black helicopters land inside the fence.

An even two dozen men dressed exactly like Claire's companion streamed out of the open side doors. There was no resistance at all from the stunned men of the cult. It was then that the whole picture coalesced into a single lucid thought.

"My e-mail," she squeaked. "It worked!"

The man walking beside her gave a thin smile.

He said, "So it was you that sent that, good thinking. If I get a chance I'll tell you how close it came to simply vanishing into obscurity but yes it worked. We owe you a big one," he said. As if broaching a delicate matter he added, "Ma'am it's clear you're not one of these people but you're still going to have to come with us. This situation comes under the heading of national security. I need to know everything you know and have your promise of silence."

Claire sighed, feeling a deep wave of relief. She wasn't exactly free and clear but like the man said these were the good guys and it was only a matter of time. In fact it was an immense relief to have someone who knew what they were doing take over.

"No problem," she said. "I've never flown in a helicopter should be fun. Oh wait a minute I left a jeep in the middle of the woods wrapped half way around a tree. My purse is in the front seat. The car belongs to one of the men they have."

This casual mention of car carnage seemed to amuse her companion. He did not quite laugh but his mouth fell open for a moment as if he were trying to describe exactly how confusing he was finding her company. Discreetly he looked her up and down as if searching for results of the accident.

"Don't worry we'll find it and fix it," he said. "We'll also bring you your bag. When did this happen? You're not hurt are you?"

"No I'm fine I wasn't going that fast. It happened this afternoon some time. I spent the last few hours hiding under a pile of leaves," she explained. "Right now I'm more than prepared to go anywhere there's a shower."

They reached the entrance of the compound. Claire was stopped by the sight of the man she knew as David St. John being removed from his cross. His body hung limply in his rescuer's arms but he was defiantly alive.

Faintly she said, "Even if I did talk about this no one would believe me. I mean, I work with material like this all the time I'm a fantasy writer. They'd just assume I'd made it up."

She glanced at her companion who still had a firm but friendly grip of her hand. He had a curious expression on his face as if he had been struck by an unusual idea.

"You look so odd," she observed. "What are you thinking?"

"I'm not completely sure. You've got me a bit distracted and trust me when I say I don't distract easily. Are you published?" he asked.

"The last couple of years have been good to me. I have two screenplays in pre-production. I think one of them will be shooting soon. I also have a novel on the New York Times best seller list," she explained. "Why?"

He raised a finger as if grasping at an unclear thought. The look in his eyes went from unfocused to focused. His finger then went to the headset he wore. For a moment it was obvious he was listening to someone speak.

"Good. Get the hostages stable and load them in chopper one. I'll be there in a moment I have another passenger. No not a prisoner a guest. Keep her under wraps but take care of her. Oh and there's a jeep in the woods it belongs to a hostage. My guest's handbag is in the front seat. Lets move people; I want this place clean by sun up."

He turned his attention back to her.

"I'm getting an interesting idea but it's kind of different. I need to clear it with my superior before I tell you. In the meantime let's get you a seat on one of those choppers."

Moving a little more deliberately now he placed a gentle but firm hand on her back and led her toward the closest one of the aircraft. As they went Claire saw Jim Young on a stretcher. An intravenous had already been placed in the back of his hand, its fluid boosting his system and staving off shock. He was being carried to the same craft. It was clear the others would soon follow.

It was a gratifying sight, one that made her feel it wouldn't be out of order to be just a little selfish.

"Will I be able to wash? I think I picked up something more than dirt when I was hiding. Every time I itch it feels like something itches back."

The man walking beside her laughed at this in a way that said he understood completely.

He said, "Trust me on this one; I know exactly how you feel. You'll have a wash and a good long sleep. Tomorrow I'll come by and we'll have our little talk. After that baring any complications you should be free to go."

*****

The ride in the helicopter was relatively short and shockingly quiet. When they landed Claire was separated from the others and brought to a small hospital room with one bed. Once there a nurse gave her a bar of strong smelling soap and told her to get into the shower and wash everywhere.

"Smells nasty I'm afraid," she said. "But if you have any passengers they'll be gone by the time you dry off."

When she returned to the room dressed in a hospital robe and gown she found her clothes were gone. Moments later the nurse who had given her the soap returned. She was carrying a syringe and small bottle in a small tray.

She said, "We're delousing your clothes. They're not that bad really but there's deer ticks up in those hills and that means Lyme disease. That can be dangerous."

Claire sat on the bed suddenly realizing how very tired she was.

"When I was hiding from the bad guys. I was a bit more concerned about them than a thing I could catch from a bug," she said.

The nurse said, "Sensible move I'd say. Hiding somewhere nasty is the sort of thing they teach you in basic training. It works."

The nurse put the tray down on the bedside table and Claire noticed a ball of cotton. She watched as the woman loaded the syringe with a dose. What it was didn't take much guessing.

"I don't think I'll need any help to sleep," Claire said. "I'm dead on my feet."

The nurse frowned slightly and said, "Oh no, this is just a general antibiotic, to counteract anything you might have picked up. Even so I want you to wait a couple of weeks then go to your personal doctor and tell him you need to be tested. Slip off your robe and give me an arm. After that I think you better lay down and cover up. You look as tired as you sound."

Claire fell asleep faster than she ever remembered doing. It made her think twice about what was really in the shot she had been given but she decided it didn't really matter. After the day she'd had a good solid sleep without dreams was like a gift.

It was the next day, exactly an hour after she'd finished her breakfast the man from the night before wandered into her room. He was wearing an anonymous looking uniform and was carrying a hard covered book. It was hers.

"I've never been a fantasy fan but this looks interesting. Can I get it autographed?" he asked.

Claire took the book and the pen he handed her and signed the inside title page.

"Who do I make it out to?" she asked.

His brows rose slightly and Claire knew that the question had been a bit silly. Real names simply didn't exist in this shadow world. When they did they were certainly not told to people like her.

"Don will do," he said.

Claire added to the signature, "for Don my hero" and gave him back the book and pen.

"You work fast. Did you really clear that machine away and have time to pick this up all since last night?"

He gave her a knowing smile and said, "Much can be done when there are many hands for the doing. That compound is as empty as a summer camp in January. We had all night after all. You should see what we can do when we're pressed for time. I also have your stuff from the hotel and your purse from the jeep. It's out in the hall. Your car is out front of the infirmary. Once we're finished our little talk one of my men will escort you to the highway. I recommend a quick trip home. After a nasty experience like this the best medicine is familiar surroundings."

Suddenly Claire realized what day it was.

"The lecture! Its Monday! I have to give a lecture at the college!"

Don shook his head smiling.

"You had two messages waiting for you at the hotel," he said. "One was from the head of the English department canceling the lecture on the grounds that you would be a bad influence on the students. Something about an unchristian attitude."

Claire remembered the woman with her sprayed hair and proper attire. The fight had ended in a draw but it seems the professor was determined to have the last word. She tried hard to be mad at the petty nature of this act but realized she simply didn't care. Don's casual attitude grew slightly guarded.

"The other message I didn't understand. I need it explained though because it sounds a bit odd. It read; Mission accomplished get your talented butt to New York."

Claire rolled her eyes at this wondering if she would ever be able to tell Jane Pendelton she almost got her star writer arrested for espionage.

"That's from my agent Jane Pendelton. She's been working her magic in my behalf. It means I've got to go to New York and sign some publishing contracts. After that I promise I'll go home."

The man in front of her looked relieved.

"I was worried for a minute there. It's probably the business I'm in but it made you look more than a little suspect," he said.

"I don't blame you," Claire said. "Can I see the others before I go?"

Don considered this requested then nodded.

"I think that can be permitted but I have to be in the room with you. They'll be released as well eventually but first they need to be what we call debriefed. In David St. Johns case that could take a while. We want to know exactly what that thing did to him."

"I bet he does too," said Claire.

Don nodded grimly and said, "He's going to need a lot of old fashioned therapy as well. They were not very civilized hosts. First things first though.

I'll bring in your things then when your dressed I'll come back with a tape recorder and some coffee. We'll have a long talk and you'll tell me everything you know from the beginning."

Claire was beginning to feel very comfortable with this mysterious professional and her strange limbo like situation. This was the part of the adventure movie they never showed you, the paperwork.

"I understand. You really don't have to worry about me you know. Like I said last night even if I did talk or write about it someday everyone would assume I made it up."

"And that's exactly how you can be of use to us," Don said. "I've talked to my superior and he agrees with me."

Claire waited for the second half of the joke but it was clear he was completely serious. Yet it didn't make sense. How could she possibly be of use to a bunch of covert agents?

"You lost me," she said. "What does he agree about?"

"Ms. Anderson the central members of this group, the men who were there last night, will spend a large part of the rest of their lives in a military prison. Most of them will never be free again. They weren't just torturing someone they were doing it with classified material. That sort of thing tends to make men in my business cranky. The problem is only the leaders and senior members were at the compound last night. There are a lot of other people that saw that machine work and most of those we can't touch without going public."

"This is something you do not want to do," Claire said.

Don tucked his autographed book under his right arm. His left hand slipped into his pocket and played with the pen she had used to sign the book.

"No we do not. We can't jail them all and if we warn them to keep silent they just might start talking out of spite," Don said.

Something occurred to Claire and she frowned as she considered the problem.

"Those other members are going to wonder what happened to the people in the compound," she said. "How do you explain that without going public?"

"Simple, we don't," Don said. "That on its own will probably scare them silent but sooner or later a few years from now the odds are someone's going to start to talk. If you write this down and it gets published then we can point at your book and say these people are just parroting something they read in a book."

Understanding hit Claire and she smiled.

"That's called disinformation isn't it?" she asked.

"Not exactly but its close," Don said.

Claire ran her mind over the things that had happened since she had watched David St. John walk down her street. It would probably be the easiest book she would ever write. The research had not simply been done but personally lived.

"I can do that," she said. "Should be fun. Though I warn you my heroine will be far more effective than I was. You'll probably find yourself being rescued in the nick of time."

He laughed at this to the point where Claire wondered what he was really laughing about.

"You were effective Ms. Anderson believe me. Your spraying that building with bullets was the best possible decision at the time. It was also very brave, or stupid, depending on how honest we're being. If my bunch hadn't happened along you all might have ended up dead anyway. They would have tracked you down and then got rid of the lot of you the old fashioned way. With a gun."

Claire knew he was probably right but she didn't understand everything he had said.

"I'm not sure I believed I or any of the men were going to get out alive. Remember I still had a lot of ground to cover to get to town. I wouldn't have made it. I wanted to make sure any deaths would leave evidence. Gun's leave evidence. What do you mean I was effective?"

Don held up fingers and itemized her success.

"Three of your shots hit their marks as far as computer hardware goes. One hit the generator. Fixable damage but it would have taken a few days. One shot hit a cultie in the leg but he'll be all right."

Claire frowned. This was not a description of a very effective action. There was something more he was not saying.

"And other than stopping the machine what does that mean," she asked.

A dry smile touched his face.

"A lot of their computer hardware is badly damaged. It'll take twenty years for our experts to figure out what goes where. They might never be able to do it particularly if the cult scientists refuse to cooperate."

"Good I'm glad," Claire said.

"So am I," Don said. "They'd only end up wanting to use it to take men like me and send them instantly around the globe to solve problems. I'd die for my country without a second thought its part of my job description. To be honest I'm not sure I want my atoms scattered over the globe. I rather like them all in one lump."

He paused for a moment thinking his own thoughts then he looked at her again.

"Will you write the book?" he asked.

Claire thought a moment. He had saved her life and the lives of three men. All he wanted in return was some of her time and talent in a way that would also profit her. It was a bargain she had no problems making.

"Don, not only will I write the thing but I'll do my damnedest to make it a best seller."

CHAPTER 26

It was casual and friendly but the little "chat" with Don turned out to be a four hour long marathon interrogation that lasted through lunch. Every moment was recorded on a small audio tape recorder. The way Don behaved Claire strongly suspected the room itself was also being videotaped. She didn't mind. She was willing to do anything it took to get her free pass home. At the same time the entire process was exhausting.

"Boy you're particular. I've worked with directors at the head of multi-million dollar film projects that were less detail obsessed," she said.

"Part of the job. What made you think of sending the e-mail to these particular naval officers?"

Once the session was over he led the way down a hospital corridor to the first of two closed and guarded doors. Behind them trailed a young man in uniform who carried Claire's luggage.

Claire followed Don into a room similar to the one she had spent the night in. Jim Young lay in a bed. He looked up at her and smiled.

He said, "Boy it's good to see you. Our host here said you were fine but I like to see things for myself."

Claire went to the bed and held his right hand gently. She had known he was hurt but seeing him bandaged, bruised and laying limply in the bed put the events of the day before into the light of harsh reality. Real life adventurers who got beat up didn't stick a bandage over it and press on. They went to the hospital, if they were lucky.

"You look a bit battered," she said wishing she could have thought of something that sounded a little less lame.

"I'm a lot battered actually but I'll be okay. Let's just say I've been here before."

"I rather guessed you had," Claire said before he could continue. "I assume whatever it was is the real reason why you ended up working at the college."

For a moment he looked at her blankly.

"How the hell did you figure that out?" he asked.

"Call it an obsession with plot," Claire explained. "It makes you fill in the blanks. Sometimes I'm wrong. Sometimes I'm right."

Jim rolled his eyes in exasperation then closed them as if the mere act of reacting to her explanation had cost him more energy than he should have expended.

"Let's just say I used to work narcotics back home and those bad boys play rough. I talked to my wife this morning. She about had a fit. Gave me flash backs of the fights we had before I gave in and said we'd move."

He shifted his position stiffly and winced as if from a strong pain. Feeling uncomfortable Claire gripped her purse like a comforting mental anchor. It made her remember one small detail.

"Jim I kind of wrecked your jeep. They found it though. It's in the garage here getting fixed," she said.

He gave her a limp smile.

"I won't be driving for a week probably two. On top of getting the piss knocked out of me I have burns on my back and behind from when they turned on that damn machine. Do you know how hard it is to find a comfortable position to lay in when everything hurts including your butt?"

Claire laughed at this and leaning against the wall near the door so did Don. Jim's smile widened slightly. He looked to Claire as if he were reliving a moment of utter disbelief.

"The lid was closing the mettle was getting hot and giving us these electric shocks. All of a sudden everything went haywire. I'm told that was you firing into the building. Whatever happened to doing what your told and running for help?"

Claire shrugged.

"Trust me if I'd thought about what I was doing through I'd have run like a scared rabbit."

Leaning against the wall Don said; "I wouldn't be too sure about that, hero's come in the funniest shapes and sizes."

He nodded toward the door. Claire accepted this silent suggestion bid Jim a quiet good bye and led the way out.

The next room had two beds. Kevin St. John, in the bed nearest the door opened his eyes and smiled weakly.

"Hi," he said.

Claire gave him a comic scowl and said, "You are a bad boy for running off alone like that."

He pouted like a sulky child and a shaky hand prodded a very purple bruise on one cheek.

"Trust me I'm paying for it," he said. Then he explained, "Turns out they had a whole series of security cameras all around the compound not just to guard against brake-ins but to look for signs that they were being watched. That's how they first spotted David."

Kevin looked across the short space between the beds at his brother. He lay like a monument, strong featured, handsome, yet even sound asleep very troubled.

"I'll be okay eventually," Kevin said. "David I'm not so sure about. I have him back alive but even when he's awake and talking he seems lost."

Don cleared his throat for attention. Claire moved so she could see both men. The strong and firmly patient security agent waited until almost reluctantly Kevin looked his way.

"I think the key word we need to concentrate on here is alive. I can't go into any details but I know more than a couple of men who've gone through a lot of stuff you don't talk about in mixed company. I've had a couple of experiences like that myself. Eventually you learned to live again but you can't learn to live if you're not alive can you?"

The man in the bed nodded his understanding and looked to his brother. Claire circled the one bed to stand by the second. Gently she laid her right hand on David's left. The hand twitched slightly and he opened his eyes. The empty exhaustion in his face was colored by a faint surprise.

He said, "It's you. Kevin told me all about you. If it weren't for you I'd be still there or dead."

His voice was a mellow tenor, soft and weak. Claire found herself wondering what he sounded like in song.

"Never wander around in front of a fantasy writer's house in the middle of the night and then vanish and expect to be ignored. We tend to be attracted to weird impossible stuff like that."

His brows raised slightly in faint surprise.

"Fantasy writer?"

"That's what I do, write books and screen plays," she explained. "When I'm not fantasizing about gorgeous men with interesting tattoos."

The surprise in David's face faded into the picture of a lost soul his brother had described.

"Right now I feel like that's all that's left. I'm a tattoo attached to a shadow that used to be a man."

Claire took David's limp hand gently in both of hers. It was cool and dry and moved just slightly to return her pressure.

She said, "Poetic but not true. Tell you what. Kevin has my address written down somewhere. You work with our host here and see what sort of damage having your atoms scattered all over the map has done to you. When you're finished you can come and visit me."

The surprise was back mixed with confusion.

"Visit you?" he asked.

"It's a quiet neighborhood near a beach in the middle of a big city. An odd combination, but it works. I've got a spare room. You can stay as long as you need to. I'm about to sign a publishing contract for a couple of books. I think I can manage room and board for one slightly battered Irishman."

She glanced toward Kevin.

"Or two if one of you doesn't mind sleeping on the sofa," she added.

Kevin shook his head.

"I don't think my girl would understand. That's one thing little brother managed to get to ahead of his big brother. I'll be married first of December. That is if they let me out of here in time."

Don said, "I think you should be out in plenty of time. David we may have to arrange a day parole for. You'll have to add me to your guest list but don't worry I clean up respectable."

"The wedding," said David. "I'd forgotten."

He looked up at her and Claire saw yet another fleeting shadow of the man that was still there under the trauma, and devastating exhaustion. The hand she held grasped hers gently.

"Could we pencil me in as a maybe?" he asked.

"No problem," Claire said. "Just don't forget okay. I've got this little story Don's asked me to write. I'll need your input."

*****

Two hours later Claire had left the state and was driving north. It was getting close to supper-time and she was wondering exactly how long she wanted to drive before she stopped for the night. Interrupting this inner debate was her cell phone. It was Jane.

She said, "Claire where on earth have you been? I got the strangest message from the publisher about that third school."

Claire smiled. At one time she might have been angry but not now. As petty as the canceling of the lecture was it represented a curiously reassuring symbol of normalcy.

"Jane I'll explain in lurid detail when I get to New York. We can put it down to if I ever do any speaking again it needs to be far away from the Bible belt. I don't know when I'll get there it might not be till tomorrow night I've been researching a new book and I'm absolutely dead."

Jane's answer was unusually quick and efficient.

"Don't drive tired you'll get into an accident. Call me when you get here after you check into a hotel and for God sakes make it a good one this time. Believe me you can afford it."

*****

The fall and winter was taken up with meticulous editing of the two books which were sold for a sum that made Claire weak at the knees. She did not forget her promise however and by spring she actually had a clear head and time enough to start the promised book.

On a warm spring evening almost a year after she watched David St. John walk down her street stark naked. She was staring at a computer screen at the word tattoo when a knock interrupted her stream of thought. She left her computer and answered the door.

It was David St. John.

"David."

He smiled. It was a sad smile, but it touched his blue eyes in a way that said he'd come far since she had last seen him and was prepared to continue the fight.

"I brought some pictures of Kevin's wedding. We both wanted to invite you but Don vetoed the idea. He said it would compromise security and he was probably right. You still open for a house guest?"

"Of course," she said expansively.

She opened the door wide and he walked in carrying a single suitcase.

"I wasn't going to come but Don told me what he'd asked you to do and why. He suggested I come and help fill in the blanks. You know, tell you about what happened to me. Besides helping you he said it would be good therapy. He might be right I don't know. Are you really turning what happened into a book?"

"Yup. When naval intelligence asks a favor of you it's not a bad idea to agree to help out, particularly when they've just saved your life. Come on in I'll make tea."

Smiling to herself Claire Anderson closed the front door and hurried to the kitchen. David wandered into the living room and stood hovering uncertainly.

"Have you done any work on it?" he asked.

Claire plugged in the kettle and came back to stand in the kitchen door. He smiled softly and there was a light in his eyes she liked very much.

"To be honest I just started thinking about it this week. I had to spend the winter taking care of old business. I've got a general outline finished but I seem to be stuck for a romantic ending."